LAURA INGALLS WILDER

Young Pioneer

Illustrated by Meryl Henderson

LAURA INGALLS WILDER

Young Pioneer

by Beatrice Gormley

ALADDIN PAPERBACKS

New York   London   Toronto   Sydney   Singapore

First Aladdin Paperbacks edition August 2001
Text copyright © 2001 by Beatrice Gormley
Illustrations copyright © 2001 by Meryl Henderson

Aladdin Paperbacks
An imprint of Simon & Schuster Children's Publishing Division
1230 Avenue of the Americas
New York, NY 10020

The text of this book was set in Adobe Garamond
Designed by Lisa Vega
Manufactured in the United States of America.

6 8 10 9 7

CIP data for this book is available from the Library of Congress.
ISBN-13: 978-0-689-83924-5
ISBN-10: 0-689-83924-3

ILLUSTRATIONS

	PAGE
Laura Ingalls Wilder, world-famous author.	5
The dry grass tickled Laura's bare feet.	14
Knitting was harder than Laura thought.	32
"Happy birthday, Half-Pint!"	48
It was the beginning of summer, time for fishing and wading.	60
The grasshoppers did come back.	70
In the evenings, by the campfire, Pa played merry songs.	89
Laura learned how to paint pictures for her sister with words.	104
Laura took her turn in the freezing lean-to, twisting hay to burn.	120
Sleigh rides in the winter.	139
She read the article aloud to Almanzo and Rose.	164
"Shall we see what he says?"	179
Honors kept on coming to Laura.	217

CONTENTS

	PAGE
The Letter	11
Laura Learns to Read	24
On to Minnesota	41
Plum Creek	53
The Saddest Time	65
Fire!	79
A Proposal of Marriage	90
Mary's Eyes	99

	PAGE
The Worst Winter	114
Miss Laura Ingalls, Teacher	126
Laura in Love	138
Rose and Rocky Ridge	149
Writing from Life	166
The Little House Books	188
"I Love You, Laura"	207

LAURA INGALLS WILDER

WILDER

Young Pioneer

The Letter

One morning at the beginning of August 1870, a hot wind rustled the grass on the Kansas prairie. In the middle of the empty plain sat a one-room log house with a barn. And inside the house, Charles Ingalls and his daughters, Laura and Mary, were getting ready to go on a picnic. The girls filled a tin pail with corn bread and fried rabbit and covered it with a napkin. Their father filled another pail with water from the well in front of the house.

Laura was excited, because they were

going to look at the Indian camp. Pa said it was safe, since the Indians had moved on. He seemed excited, too.

Ma was staying home. She moved slowly these days, as if her big belly slowed her down. Now she sat in her rocking chair by the window, her head bent over the shirt she was mending.

Pausing in the doorway of the log house, Pa settled his wide-brimmed straw hat on his head. "Well, Caroline," he said to his wife, "Mrs. Robertson's on her way. And we're on ours."

Ma smiled at them. "Be sure to wear your sunbonnet, Laura."

Laura took her calico sunbonnet from a peg near the door. Of course Ma didn't have to remind Laura's obedient older sister. Mary's sunbonnet was already on her head, with its strings tied neatly under her chin.

The Indian camp was a long way across the prairie from the Ingallses' log house. Since

Laura was only three and a half and small for her age, she rode on the back of their big bulldog, Jack.

"Don't ever try to ride on any other dog, will you, girls," warned Pa as he lifted Laura onto Jack's muscled back. "Jack only lets you ride because he loves you."

Mary, five and a half, walked beside Pa. The sun beat down on their backs, and the insects hummed in the grass all around them. The wind lifted Pa's brown beard and stirred the ends of Mary's blond braids and Laura's brown ones. The dry grass tickled Laura's bare feet as she rode.

"I don't see the camp, Pa," said Laura.

"You can't see it from here, Half-Pint," he answered. "But we know we're walking toward it." He pointed a little to the right. "There's our landmark, those bluffs on the northwest horizon."

With the end of summer, the prairie had turned brown. The prairie *smelled* brown,

too—like a loft full of hay. In the spring, the new grass had smelled rich and green, and the wind had swished softly through it.

When the sun was overhead, the restless wind died away. Glancing over her shoulder, Laura saw two dots in the distance—their house and barn. "Here we are," said Pa, and Laura turned back to see that they were at the edge of a hollow in the flat land.

"The Indians pitch their camp in the hollow to get out of the wind," said Pa. "See the bushes growing down here? The hollow shelters them, and the bushes give wood for the Indians' fires." He pointed to the blackened places where the Indians had built their fires. "And the hollow shelters the fires, too."

The Ingalls family's house on the prairie was in Indian Territory, where the Osage Indians were still living. Sometimes Osage men with shaved heads and scalp locks of hair and feathers came to the log house. They helped themselves to the Ingallses' food and tobacco, but they never actually did any harm. Still, Laura and Mary were afraid of these wild-looking men.

Today, with Pa and Jack right beside her, Laura felt safe. Pa and Mary and Laura sat under a bush and ate their lunch. It was lovely for her and Mary to have Pa all to themselves for an afternoon—usually he worked in the fields all day, or went out hunting.

After they finished eating, Laura was afraid they would have to head back for home, but Pa said, "Let's see what we can see around the camp." He showed the girls the moccasin footprints around the campfires, and the bones left over from the deer the Indians had eaten. Jack sniffed the bones carefully, then chose one and carried it into the shade of a sumac bush to gnaw.

Meanwhile, the girls were delighted to discover colored beads scattered here and there on the ground of the campsite. There were red ones and blue ones, green ones and white ones and brown ones. "Did the beads fall off their moccasins, Pa?" asked Laura.

"Maybe they spilled from an Indian girl's workbag," said Mary. Mary had her own workbag for her sewing, like Ma, and she was very proud of it.

"Maybe you're both right," said Pa. "I wonder how many you can find?" The girls filled the pockets of their faded calico dresses.

Before they knew it, the sun was low in the west. It would soon be milking time. Pa lifted Laura onto Jack's back again. "*You're* a little Indian," he teased her, "riding without saddle or bridle."

By the time they reached home, the sky was turning pink behind them. Laura ran into the log house to show Ma her beads.

But inside the door, Laura stopped short. The woman stirring a pot at the fireplace was Mrs. Robertson, who had come to visit Ma. And there was a man sitting in Ma's rocking chair, Dr. Tann. Laura had seen the doctor, a black man, once before, when the whole family was sick with malaria.

Ma smiled at them from her bed in the corner by the fireplace. "Mary—Laura—come see your new sister."

"Oh!" said Laura and Mary at the same time. It had already been a day of adventures—a picnic with Pa, and seeing the Indian camp, and finding the beads—and now a new sister?

Stepping up to the bed with Mary, Laura saw a tiny baby lying in the crook of Ma's arm. "This is Caroline Celestia," said Ma. "I wrote her name in the family Bible, after your names. We'll call her Carrie."

"She's so little," breathed Laura. "Can she play?"

The grown-ups laughed, and Ma said, "Not just yet. But soon she'll be big enough to play with you and Mary. And I know you'll be kind, patient big sisters and help me take good care of her."

"*I* will," said Mary quickly. "I helped take care of Laura, when she was born in the Big Woods."

Laura never liked it when Mary talked like that, like a grown-up. But at least now Laura would be able to talk the same way to Carrie.

Not long after Carrie was born, Pa hitched the horses to the wagon and drove off to town. There he'd buy the things the family didn't grow or make themselves: cornmeal, sugar, salt pork. He'd also mail Ma's letter to the folks back in Wisconsin. The town of Independence was thirteen miles away, and he was gone for two days.

Pa usually came home from town full of news and stories, his eyes twinkling. But this time, his blue eyes were sober. That night, after Laura and Mary had put on their red flannel nightgowns and said their prayers and snuggled into bed together, Laura heard her parents talking. It sounded like they were thinking of leaving the prairie. The land their house was built on was part of the Osage Indian Reserve, and so it did not really belong to them.

"Charles, our house that you built with logs you hauled from the creek bottoms!" said Ma. "And all your labor to dig the well."

"I know, Caroline," said Pa. "And we have the cow and calf in the barn, and the sod's broken for next spring's planting."

Laura wanted very badly to ask, "If we left, where would we go?" But children should not interrupt when grown-ups were talking. Children should not even listen to grown-ups' talk, when they should be sleeping instead.

Luckily, Ma asked Pa the same question. "Although it might be for the best if we did go," Ma added. "What if there was a prairie fire in another year or so, after you'd planted wheat? We'd lose it all." The two voices murmured on and on, and nothing was decided that night.

A few days later, their neighbor Mr. Robertson came back from his trip to town and brought Pa a letter. Laura and Mary couldn't read yet, but they knew that letters were important. When Pa or Ma opened one of those folded pieces of paper, they found things out. Letters came from Wisconsin, where the Ingallses used to live in the Big Woods—from Grandma, or Aunt Eliza, or Aunt Martha. Ma would read the letters out loud, and then they would know the news about the aunts and uncles and cousins in Wisconsin.

Pa's new letter was from Wisconsin, but it wasn't from the relatives. It was from Mr. Gustafson, the man who had bought the house in the Big Woods from Pa before they moved to the prairie.

A hopeful look came over Pa's face as he ran his eyes across the paper. "Gustafson says he can't make the payments on the house," he said. "We can have it back. So there's a home waiting for us in Pepin."

Ma's face lit up. "Home, back with the folks," she said softly. "They haven't even seen our Baby Carrie." She turned to Laura and Mary. "Girls, how would you like to go back to the house where you were born?"

"Oh, I would like that so much!" said Mary. "I remember our house in the Big Woods."

Laura wished *she* could say she remembered that house where she was born, but she couldn't. She loved the snug house Pa had built for them here, and she loved the prairie. Still, if Ma and Pa and Mary were happy about going back to the Big Woods, it must be a wonderful place.

Pa was already outside, fastening the canvas cover back on the wagon. Mary and Laura helped carry their things out to be packed. The next morning, the early sunlight streamed past Pa and Ma on the wagon seat, through the gathered circle of the cover, and into the front of the wagon, where Laura and

Mary rode. In the back, Baby Carrie slept on the bedding. Now the wagon, not the log house, was home for the Ingalls family until they reached Wisconsin.

Laura Learns
to Read

On the long trip back to Wisconsin, the fall rains began. At a few of the river crossings, there were bridges or ferries. But in many places, the wagon track just stopped on one bank of the river and started on the other side. As the water level rose, these fords became more dangerous to cross. At one river, Pa had to swim, leading the horses, while Ma took the reins.

That scared all of them, even Pa, and they didn't try to cross the next swollen river. Instead, Pa stopped at a large farm and got work with the farmer. There was an extra cabin on the farm, where they could live until the river went down a bit.

One day when Pa was out working, the cabin chimney caught on fire. The main part of the chimney was stone, but the top was only mud-plastered sticks. Ma ran outside to knock the burning sticks off the chimney, leaving Baby Carrie in Mary's lap. A blazing stick fell down the chimney, right in front of the rocker where Mary sat with the baby. Mary was too frightened to move, but Laura grabbed the back of the rocker and dragged her sisters away from danger.

"Why, Half-Pint, I didn't know you were so strong," said Pa when he came home that evening. "Strong and brave," agreed Ma. "And not even four years old." Ma's brown eyes and Pa's blue eyes shone at Laura, and she felt very proud.

Soon afterward, the river went down. They loaded the wagon again, crossed the river, and traveled on and on. "Now we're in Missouri," Ma said, and some days later, "Now we're in Iowa." Laura began to think that they'd lived in the covered wagon as long as they'd lived on the Kansas prairie.

They left the flat prairie, and the wagon climbed up hills and down into valleys. More and more trees appeared, until there were trees all around with their branches arching over the wagon track. On the prairie there were trees only in the creek bottoms, far from the log house.

Mary leaned out of the front of the wagon and said, "Ma, we're in the Big Woods now, aren't we?"

Ma, holding Baby Carrie on her lap, spoke over her shoulder. "Yes. We aren't far from Grandma and Grandpa's. We'll stay with them tonight."

Laura was quiet. She didn't remember these trees and trees and trees and trees the way Mary seemed to. She wasn't sure she remembered Grandma, either.

That evening, Pa halted the horses outside a big house, and an older woman hurried out, wiping her hands on her apron. Her eyes sparkled as she hugged each of them, and Laura thought maybe she did remember Grandma's face. Or was it that her expression was something like Pa's?

Grandma and Grandpa had plenty of room—one big room and two bedrooms—even though Pa's younger sister Ruby still lived with them. Pa and Ma and Laura and Mary stayed there for a few days, then for a longer time with Uncle Henry and Aunt Polly Quiner and their children. All these relatives looked a little familiar to Laura, too. And everyone was so comfortable together, it wasn't like being with strangers.

In the evenings Pa would get out his fiddle and play, and everyone sang. Or they told stories. Pa told the best stories, and the relatives especially wanted to hear about Kansas. So

Pa told about the time the wolf pack surrounded him when he was riding his horse Patty, and the time he heard a panther scream and thought it was their neighbor, Mrs. Robertson. He told about the time Indians came right into their house and made Ma bake corn bread for them.

Laura was having such a good time with the relatives that she wasn't sure she wanted to stop visiting. But finally the day came when Pa, Ma, Mary, Laura, and Carrie got into the wagon once more. They drove up a ridge and into a clearing dotted with tree stumps. Inside a rail fence were two beautiful oak trees with deep, rich reddish-brown leaves, and behind them, a small log house with a window on each side of the door.

Laura gazed at the log house, and the house seemed to gaze back at her with its two glass windows. The way Laura felt about the house was the same way she had felt about Grandma: She didn't exactly remember the

Ingallses' house in the Big Woods, but something about it was familiar and comfortable.

Trees and trees and trees and trees! Laura stood in the yard in front of the Ingallses' cabin, her face turned up to the clouds of colored leaves all around. She was used to the treeless prairie, where the brightest colors were in the sky, at sunset and sunrise. Here, the whole woods was colors: brilliant orange, and dark red, and glowing yellow that looked like sunshine even though the sky was gray.

The colors made Laura want to run through the woods, scattering fallen leaves and shouting. But Ma had told Mary and Laura to stay in the yard, inside the rail fence. There were wild bears in the woods, and wolves, and panthers. Children who wandered into the woods might get lost, and they might never find their way home again.

If Jack were here, thought Laura, she would

feel safe in the woods with him. But they had a new black and white dog, Wolf. He was young, and it would take him a long time to learn to be as good a watchdog as Jack.

Inside the Ingallses' yard in the Big Woods there were only two trees. "This tree will be my house," said Mary, patting the trunk of one of the big oaks.

"And this will be mine," said Laura. She was glad they lived in a place where she and Mary could each have their own beautiful tree.

The Ingallses' house in the Big Woods of Wisconsin was actually more comfortable than their house on the Kansas prairie. The prairie house had only one room—this house had a big room *and* a bedroom. And upstairs was an attic where Mary and Laura could play in cold weather.

The weather was getting colder every day as the leaves fell from the trees and let the sky show through the bare branches. Pa was often out with his rifle, hunting deer and bear. One day he went to Uncle Henry's (Ma's brother) to help him butcher a hog, and he came home with spareribs for dinner.

The first snow fell, and their cat, Black Susan, stayed indoors by the cookstove most of the time. Laura and Mary had to stay indoors, too. Ma taught Mary to knit, and Mary worked on a scarf for her doll. "May I knit, too?" Laura begged.

Ma thought she was too young, but she found some scraps of yarn and let her try. "I want to make mittens for my baby sister," said Laura. She leaned over to make a bright face at Carrie, sitting on Ma's lap. Carrie laughed. Laura could make her laugh better than anyone, except Pa.

Knitting was harder than Laura had thought. The needles and the yarn seemed to want to go their own ways. But in a few days, a little mitten began to grow on Laura's needles.

Wolf crouched in front of Laura and nudged her foot with his nose. "I can't play now, Wolf," she told him. "I'm knitting mittens for Baby Carrie."

After days of labor, Laura finally finished the mitten. "I'm through!"

"Very nice work, Laura." Ma held the pink mitten up to the light from the window. "But this is only half a pair of mittens. Carrie has two little hands—you don't want one of them to be cold, do you?"

"No . . ." But Laura also didn't want to sit back down and struggle with the needles and yarn anymore. "Couldn't you knit the other mitten, Ma?"

Ma shook her head. "We must always finish what we begin. Let's cast on the stitches for the second mitten."

So again, Laura worked every afternoon for days and days. The second mitten seemed to take twice as long. What a moment when finally Ma slipped the little thing off Laura's needles and Laura put it on Baby Carrie's hand! Now, for the first mitten . . . where was it?

"What is Wolf doing?" Mary pointed toward the bedroom. The dog had squeezed under Ma and Pa's bed, with only his black and white hind legs and his wagging tail sticking out.

"My land!" exclaimed Ma. Wolf was backing out from under the bed with something pink and stringy in his mouth.

"You took Baby Carrie's mitten!" Laura told him. "Bad dog!" Now she would have to spend even more dreary afternoons knitting Carrie's mitten again. It was too awful to think about, and she burst into tears.

"Hush, Laura." Ma shifted Carrie to one side of her lap and put her arm around Laura. "You ought to be glad, not crying. Haven't you learned to knit?"

Laura's sobs trailed off, and she nodded.

"Besides," Ma went on, "you finished

what you started. That was even more important than learning to knit." Setting Carrie down for a moment, she took Wolf by the scruff of his neck and pried the yarn from his mouth. "No harm done. I can wash this yarn and dry it and knit it into a mitten again in no time."

Laura's tears dried up as she realized what Ma meant. Laura *didn't* have to knit the mitten all over again! She gave Wolf a hug, to show they were friends after all.

Mary turned six that winter, in January 1871, and Laura turned four on February seventh. For her birthday she got her first real doll, a rag doll with button eyes and black yarn hair. Laura was overjoyed. Now she and Mary could play together with their dolls, dressing and undressing them, and teaching them to knit, and making them be very good and quiet on Sundays.

Sundays were long, dull days, except when

Ma read to Mary and Laura from the big Bible. "Please read our names, Ma," begged Laura.

"Why, Laura, you and Mary already know your names." Ma smiled at her, but she turned to the middle of the Bible, where there were pages for family records. "'Births,'" she read. "'Mary Amelia Ingalls born Tuesday, January 10th, 1865.'"

Laura put a finger on the fourth line of the page. She knew that was her name. Ma read, "'Laura Elizabeth Ingalls born Thursday, February 7th, 1867.'"

Laura sighed happily. It was so satisfying to think of *her* name in that big, important book.

Late in the winter they went to visit Uncle Charles and Aunt Martha Carpenter, Ma's older sister. One day Mary and Laura went to school with their cousins, Letty and Will and Joe. At recess, the children threw snowballs at one another, and Gus, one of the older boys, grabbed the smaller children to rub their faces in the snow. "Run, Laura!" shouted Cousin Letty. "That bully Gus will get you!"

Too late—Gus had already seized Laura from behind, by her shoulders. He pushed her face into a snowbank, and she couldn't see. But she could feel his thumb digging into her shoulder, and she turned her head and bit that thumb as hard as she could.

Suddenly Laura was free, and Gus was dancing around the schoolyard, shaking drops of blood from his thumb onto the snow and yelling. Cousin Will laughed. "Well, Gus, I guess you've learned to leave Laura alone!"

In springtime, when the weather turned warm again, Laura and Mary took their dolls outdoors to the two big oak trees in front of their house. Then summer came, and Ma thought Mary was old enough to walk to the Barry Corner School. "It's time you learned to read, Mary."

The first morning, Laura watched Mary leave with her schoolbook under her arm, swinging a bright tin lunch pail. Laura longed to go with her. "I want to learn to read, too," she said.

Ma said Laura wasn't old enough to go to school. "But you can learn your letters now, at home."

So in the evenings after dinner, when Ma went over Mary's lessons with her, Laura learned along with Mary. Soon Laura could say the whole alphabet. She learned to read her own name, and to sound out words.

One day, the words on a page of Mary's reader came together before Laura's eyes with a snap. "'The . . . Sto-ry—The Story. The Story . . . of . . . Laura'! Ma, I'm reading!"

Laura turned back to the page, eager to read more of this story about her. "'Laura . . . was . . . a . . .'" Here came a strange word. "'. . . a glut-ton.' Ma, what is a glutton?"

Ma explained that a glutton was a greedy

person who ate too much food. Mary, who was practicing writing her letters, smiled down at her slate.

Laura stared at the page, shocked. "*Am* I greedy, Ma?" Her voice trembled.

"Laura, the story doesn't mean *you*. There are many little girls in the world named Laura. Think of the Lauras we know."

"Grandma is Laura," Mary spoke up. "And Aunt Docia's first name is Laura."

"And Cousin Laura," admitted Laura. She had met that other Laura at a dance at Grandma's, and she didn't like her.

Ma was still talking, explaining that Laura didn't need to be a glutton, if she didn't want to. Laura felt better. Maybe Cousin Laura was a glutton.

Now and then in the summer there were thunderstorms. One night, a terrible storm raged right over the Ingallses' house. Laura woke up at a crack and a boom that hurt her ears, followed by a ripping noise.

When Laura looked out the front window the next morning, one of the two beautiful oak trees had a black scar down its side. "Oh, Mary! Your tree—your house!" Even though it was Mary's tree, not hers, it hurt Laura to see the oak so damaged.

On to Minnesota

In the spring of 1873, Uncle Peter (Pa's brother) and Aunt Eliza (Ma's sister) and their children came to visit. At suppertime, Pa and Uncle Peter talked about moving west.

"It's getting so there are more houses than trees in these woods," said Pa.

"They say in town that the railroad is going right out through Minnesota," said Uncle Peter. "That means a farmer on the Minnesota prairie could make a good living, because he could get his wheat to market in the East."

Laura knew what a *railroad* was—a special track for a special kind of wagon—but she had never seen one. Neither had Mary.

Pa and Uncle Peter went on talking about how much easier farming on the prairie would be than farming in the woods. "No trees to cut down! No stumps and rocks to dig out! No hills! Just acres of rich, flat soil."

Harvest time came, and Uncle Henry and Pa helped each other cut their oats as they had the year before. But that harvest would be the last one for the Ingallses in the Big Woods of Wisconsin. Next spring, in 1874, they and Uncle Peter and Aunt Eliza would head west for Minnesota.

Meanwhile, Pa sold the house and the land. Neighbors would keep Black Susan the cat and Wolf the dog, Pa said. But he sold the cow, Sukey, to a family in town. Laura was already sad at the thought of leaving Black Susan and Wolf. The day a strange man led Sukey off down the road, she had to blink hard to keep back the tears.

The next day, though, when the Ingalls family climbed into the wagon with all their belongings, Laura forgot about being sad. There was so much to look forward to. First they would visit with Grandpa and Grandma Ingalls for a week or two. Then they'd move on to Uncle Peter and Aunt Eliza's house, to spend the winter with Alice, Peter, Ella, Lansford, and their new little cousin, Baby Edith. What could be more fun than that?

It was a wonderful winter, especially playing in the snow with the cousins. But toward the end of January, they all came down with scarlet fever. Laura was the last child to get sick, and she seemed to get the scarlet fever worse than the rest of them.

With scarlet fever, there was no playing in the snow, or anywhere else. The children had to stay in bed and be quiet and take nasty medicine from Ma's big spoon, even when they started to feel better. As for Laura, she felt so weak and awful that she didn't mind staying in bed, for once. That was a strange time, when she seemed to sleep when everyone else was awake, and lie awake when they were asleep.

One night, when all the other children were breathing slowly and peacefully, Laura listened to the grown-ups talking in the next room. "I think the children are well enough to travel now," said Aunt Eliza.

"All except Laura," said Ma.

"You're the nurse, Caroline," said Pa, "but we can't wait much longer. It's February already. The ice on Lake Pepin might hold, or it might not. The lake is part of the Missouri River, so the water's always trying to break the ice up and move downstream."

Laura drifted off, but in her half-dreamy mind she imagined the river like a herd of wild horses. They surged downstream, crushing the ice under their hooves.

❈ ❈ ❈ ❈

The grown-ups packed most of the household that night, and they got up very early the next morning to pack the rest. Nothing was left unpacked except Laura on the bed.

"Now we'll pack you up, too, dearie," said Aunt Eliza merrily. She and Ma let Laura keep her red flannel nightgown on, but they dressed her over her nightgown in a coat and hood and mittens and woolen stockings, and Ma wound a soft, warm scarf around her throat. Then they bundled her up in blankets with only her face peeping out as if she were Baby Edith, only much larger. Pa carried her out to where the horses and bobsleds waited under the gray sky.

Laura was snug and warm, but it bothered her to be so wrapped up that she could hardly move her arms and legs. And she was facing backwards, so she could see only a little scrap of the world beyond the blanket. The snow swished under the bobsled runners, and the horses' harness jingled as they trotted down the long road to the lake.

Once the two bobsleds reached the lake, they drove straight out onto the ice. All Laura could see was a small section of shoreline, with its bare trees and the buildings of Pepin getting smaller and smaller. The snow swished, the harness jingled. No one talked.

Laura had almost drifted off to sleep when she heard a new sound. Then she was wide awake, with her heart beating fast. *Splash*. *Splash*. " . . . the water's always trying to break the ice up . . . ," Pa had said last night.

Was the ice breaking up now? It was because of Laura, because she was still sick, that they had waited too long, and any minute the heavy bobsleds packed with all their things would crash through the ice. "Pa!" she wailed, struggling to turn around. "Ma! There's water—"

Then Ma's arm was around her, Ma's hand was patting her through the blankets, and Ma's gentle voice spoke close to her head. "It's all right, Laura. It's just a little water on top of the ice. The ice is good and thick underneath."

Laura must have gone to sleep then. She woke up in a bed, in a hotel on the other side of Lake Pepin. Pa was sitting on the edge of the bed. He looked tired, but he was smiling and holding out a book. "Happy birthday, Half-Pint! I'll wait until you get well to give you your birthday spanks this year."

"Oh, Pa!" Laura had forgotten about her birthday. She opened the book wonderingly. *The Floweret*, it was called, and it was all verses. She read the first one out loud, stumbling over a word here and there, but listening to the rhymes chiming like bells. "Thank you, Pa!"

Laura couldn't wait to read *her* book to Carrie. And she would generously let Mary borrow *her* book. What a day! She was seven, and they had all crossed the Missouri River safely. And she was holding a book of her own.

* * * *

The two Ingalls families moved on the next day, but before long the spring thaw of 1874 had started. There wasn't enough snow for bobsleds, the roads were deep in mud that wagon wheels would get stuck in, and the creeks were roaring with melted snow water. The travelers stopped on the east bank of a creek, where Uncle Peter found an empty house.

Aunt Eliza wondered if the house had been abandoned because it was in danger of being washed away. It was right on the edge of the creek—in fact, the water ran through the cellar, in one end and out the other. But Pa and Uncle Peter said the house was built on rock, so there was no danger.

Laura liked that house. She and Mary and the cousins would lift up the trapdoor to watch the water rushing through the cellar. They pretended they were on a ship. In the evening, when Pa brought out his fiddle, Laura begged him to play "Sailing, Sailing,

Over the Bounding Main." In their beds on the floor, the children heard the water gurgling as they fell asleep, still pretending they were on a ship at sea.

One of those nights, Laura lay awake after Mary had gone to sleep. The bedroom door was open a little, showing the firelight flickering in the other room where Pa and Ma and Uncle Peter and Aunt Eliza were sitting. Pa was playing his fiddle, a song so beautiful that it made Laura's throat hurt.

Suddenly she remembered something she hadn't thought about since she came down with scarlet fever. While they were still at Uncle Peter's, there were the nicest icicles hanging from the eaves of the roof. The children knocked them down with the broom handle and ate them, until Ma told them not to eat anymore. "So much ice isn't good for your insides."

Laura meant to mind Ma, but then she saw one more beautiful piece of icicle lying in the snow, like a long, shining stick of candy. When Aunt Eliza called the children in to supper, Laura popped the last piece of the icicle in her mouth to hide it.

"Laura, are you eating ice?" asked Ma.

Laura had to swallow the ice in order to answer. "No, ma'am."

Now, in bed with Pa's fiddle singing and the firelight dancing in the next room, with her peaceful family all around, Laura felt as cold inside as if the icicle she'd swallowed was still there. She had told her first lie—and she had hardly noticed it!

Laura felt a loud sob rise up from the cold lump inside her. Pa's fiddle stopped, and Ma slipped through the door and stooped beside Laura. "What is it? Did you have a bad dream?"

"Oh, Ma!" Laura buried her head in Ma's skirt.

"Shh, don't wake the others," said Ma gently.

Laura went on more quietly, but she

couldn't stop crying. "Everything's lovely—but me! Everyone's good—but me! I lied about the ice."

"Ice?" Ma sounded puzzled. "What ice?"

Ma didn't seem to remember about the icicles, so Laura had to explain. Her face burned with shame as she remembered all over again how quickly she had lied, and how trusting Ma's face had looked, believing her.

"Well, Laura," said Ma, "I forgive you. I know you won't tell me an untruth again."

Laura thought she had never heard a sound as lovely as Ma's quiet voice at that moment. Tucked in once more, Laura listened to Pa's fiddle again and watched the firelight through drowsy eyelids. The music sounded even sweeter, and the dancing light and shadows were even more beautiful. And she was part of it all, and at peace.

Plum Creek

Springtime brought soft air and fresh green grass, and the creek went down. The Ingalls families packed up the wagons again and started west. Only Uncle Peter and Aunt Eliza and Cousins Alice, Peter, Ella, Lansford, and Edith were going just a little way farther, to a farm on the Zumbro River. There they said good-bye, and Laura and her family drove on west in their covered wagon.

Laura was sorry to leave the cousins, but she was happy to be outside in the warm weather, with the country growing more beautiful each day. Every night Pa would find some pleasant place to camp, near a spring or creek. One of those evenings, just as Laura was settling down to sleep in the wagon, she heard a long, clear, haunting call. "What was that?" she asked.

"It's the whistle of a railroad engine," answered Ma from the campfire. "Look quickly, and you can see it."

Scrambling to the front of the wagon, Laura poked her head out. The sun had just gone down, but it was still light enough to see the railroad bridge over the creek. As she watched, the engine, wearing its smokestack like a huge topknot, burst into view. It was hauling a whole train of cars. Smoke billowing from its smokestack, the train clattered across the bridge.

After the train had disappeared, Pa said, "We are living in a great age. Do you know that a train covers more distance in a day than an ox team can travel in a week? And now there are railroad tracks from one side of the country to the other. That happened only a few years ago, when we were still living in Kansas."

That summer, 1874, Charles and Caroline Ingalls and their three girls arrived at Walnut Grove, one of the new railroad towns in western Minnesota. They bought a dugout house and 172 acres of land on nearby Plum Creek.

Their nearest neighbors were the Nelsons. Laura liked to visit them, because Mrs. Nelson had only one baby, and she wasn't as busy as Ma. Mrs. Nelson taught Laura to milk the Nelsons' gentle old cow. After Laura had practiced for a while, the cow would switch her tail and push Laura away with one hoof, but always gently so as not to hurt her.

Then Mrs. Nelson would finish milking while the barn cats sat watching her and purring. After she was through, Mrs. Nelson set the milk bucket on the ground for them. The first time this happened, Laura tried to shoo the cats away. Black Susan, their cat in the Big Woods of Wisconsin, was not allowed to drink milk from anything except her own cracked saucer.

"Let them be," Mrs. Nelson told Laura. "The poor cats want their milk."

Laura let the cats be. Ma would not think it was—well, *clean*—to let cats drink from the milk bucket. But Ma would also think it was very rude if a child like Laura argued with a grown-up.

By the time the Ingallses moved to Plum Creek, it was too late to plant a wheat crop that year. But Pa went to work for Mr. Nelson to earn money for seed and a plow. He planned to break the sod on his land that fall and plant wheat next spring. A bumper crop could make their fortune, Pa said.

In the fall, Mary and Laura were almost

ten and almost eight, and it was time for them both to go to school. Every day they walked the two miles from their house by the creek to the school in town. They made new friends at school, like Anna Ensign (Mary's age) and her brother Howard (Laura's age).

Mary and Laura loved their teacher, and they liked seeing other children every day. If only the other children hadn't included a girl named Nellie Owens! Nellie was as pretty as a store-bought doll, with yellow curls and blue eyes. But she *acted* ugly.

At lunchtime the first day, the children took their tin lunch pails out in the schoolyard as usual. Nellie looked around to see what everyone was eating. "Homemade bread and butter—is that all you have for lunch, Laura? *I* have boughten crackers and cheese. My father's the storekeeper, you know—Owens' Dry Goods. He makes lots of money, and he lets me have all the candy I want."

Laura watched Nellie dig a handful of shiny hard candy, red and green striped, from her lunch pail. Laura and Mary got store candy only once a year, in their Christmas stockings.

Smiling, Nellie walked around the group of children, her golden curls dangling as she bent to give each one a piece of candy. But she didn't offer any to Mary or Laura. Howard, sitting next to Laura on the grass, held out his piece of striped candy. "You can have mine, Laura."

Laura wanted the candy, but she felt too proud to take it. "I don't want any candy from such a mean, stuck-up girl."

"But it's my candy, now—please?" Howard looked as if he really did want Laura to take it. So finally she bit it in half, and they shared. Nellie noticed, and she didn't look pleased.

Winter passed, and spring came. Pa planted a large field of wheat. He knew that grasshoppers had eaten the crops last year, but he was hoping this year would be different. But the grasshoppers returned and ate the wheat fields bare.

Laura knew her parents were worried, but she couldn't help being happy just to be eight years old and living on Plum Creek. It was the beginning of the summer, time for fishing and wading.

One hot Saturday afternoon, Laura and Mary were down at the big pool in the creek. They were expecting Nellie Owens to visit, but meanwhile they were fishing. Laura already had her line in the water with a fat worm on the hook.

"Laura?" Mary held out her hook. "Would you please?"

Mary was squeamish about worms. She turned her face away as Laura baited her

hook. Then they sat on the bank with their feet dangling in the pool. Reflections of the willow trees shimmered on the quiet water at the far end of the pool.

After a little while, Mary said, "Laura . . . I know Nellie is mean. She's the meanest, most stuck-up girl I ever knew. But do you think we ought to . . . it doesn't seem right to invite her here and then frighten her."

"Why not?" asked Laura. "Nellie invited us to her house and wouldn't even let us touch her boughten doll with the eyes that open and shut. She wouldn't let us play with any of her toys." Mary didn't argue with that.

A few minutes later, Nellie appeared. "What a pretty white dress, Nellie," said Laura. To herself she thought how silly it was to wear a nice dress to play at the creek on a Saturday. Laura and Mary wore their oldest, patched dresses. And Nellie was wearing *shoes,* too! "Would you like to fish? I'll put a worm on your hook for you."

Nellie shuddered and turned up her nose. "I guess country girls go fishing, but I wouldn't."

"Let's wade in the pool, then," said Mary. She put down her fishing line and stepped into the water.

Laura waded into the pool, too, smiling to herself—Mary was going along with her plan. "Ooh, the water feels so good, Nellie! Wouldn't you like to take off your shoes and cool your feet?"

Nellie went in gingerly at first, holding up the starched white skirt of her dress. Then she tucked the skirt into her sash and waded in farther. Laura let her enjoy the pool for a few moments before she screamed, "Watch out, Nellie! The crab! Run!"

Looking all around, Nellie screamed, "Where? I don't see the crab!"

"That big old crab with great big claws! Right behind you! Run for the willows!" Laura pointed to the muddy end of the pool.

Nellie dashed into the mud, splashing. She

stayed there for several minutes, even after Laura and Mary assured her that the crab was gone. When she came out, her legs were covered with leeches—dark, mud-colored, worm-like things that sucked blood from your skin.

At suppertime, Ma asked Laura and Mary why Nellie had run home screaming. Laura told the truth, choking back her laughter.

"Girls," said Ma in her gentle but firm voice, "you must not tease your guests."

Pa said nothing, but his blue eyes twinkled.

When the cold winter winds started to blow that fall, the Ingalls family moved into town. They rented a small house behind the church. From there, Mary and Laura could walk to school, even in the snow. And it would be safer for Ma to be in town, because she would need help when she had the new baby she was expecting.

One day Laura and Mary came home from school to find a neighbor woman at the stove, and Ma in bed. She looked tired, but very happy. "Come see your baby brother," she told the girls.

A boy in the family! Laura was so excited. After that she and Mary ran home from school every day to look at the baby. They called him Freddie. Ma wrote his full name, Charles Frederick Ingalls, and his date of birth, November 1st, 1875, in the family Bible.

The Saddest Time

During the spring thaw of 1876, Ma was sick. Laura and Mary were frightened, and Laura could see that Pa was worried, too. One morning he told her to run to the Nelsons'. "Tell Mr. Nelson to go to town and send a telegram for a doctor." The doctor would have to come to Walnut Grove on the train from another town.

Laura ran as fast as she could, down the path to the creek. The Nelsons lived on the other side. There was a footbridge from one bank to the other—except today there was no sign of the creek banks. The creek was a torrent of yellow, foaming water rushing over the barely visible footbridge.

Laura didn't want to go on, but Pa had told her to run to the Nelsons'. Ma needed a doctor. Laura waded into the water, feeling for each step on the wooden bridge. The creek roared all around, making her dizzy with the noise.

When the water was up to Laura's knees, she thought she heard a human voice through the roar of the water. "Go back!"

Laura paused and looked up at the far bank. It was Mr. Nelson, swinging his arms as if to push her away. She could read his lips, "You'll drown!"

Standing with the yellow water swirling around her knees, Laura shouted back at the top of her lungs, "Ma's awfully sick! Pa says to please go to town and telegraph for the doctor."

Laura had to repeat her words twice, each time screaming as loud as she possibly could.

Then Mr. Nelson nodded and held up one finger—finally he had understood. He turned and hurried back up the bank to go to town.

For just a moment Laura was relieved and happy. Then, as she tried to turn around, her foot slipped on the plank. In an instant Laura was sprawled in the flooded creek. Without thinking, she clutched the plank with her arms and legs. The cold, muddy water roared all around her, trying to drag her away.

"Help!" shouted Laura, choking. It was foolish to call for help. No one could hear her above the roar of the water. And no one could see her. Mr. Nelson was on his way to town. Pa and Ma and Mary and Carrie were all in the house.

Slowly Laura inched along the plank, back the way she had come. She kept her head turned downstream so the water didn't splash into her nose. She didn't dare try to stand up. Slowly, slowly she crawled forward toward solid ground.

At last Laura reached the bank. It was muddy, but solid. Her arms and legs were trembling, and she had to rest for a moment before she could stand up.

When Laura came into the house, Pa was at Ma's side, holding her up to drink some tea. It was only when he stood up that he noticed Laura. "You're dripping wet! What happened?"

Her teeth chattering, Laura told him about the flooded creek.

"By jinks!" said Pa. He hugged Laura close. "You're a brave girl. Thank the Lord you're safe."

The next day, the doctor came. Ma got well, and the creek went down. Mary and Laura went back to school. Freddie grew bigger, and he started to smile, then sit up, and then crawl. That spring, Pa planted another wheat crop, but only a small one, in case the grasshoppers came back.

Pa said that 1876 was a very important

year, because the United States of America would be one hundred years old on the Fourth of July. Laura liked to think about that. "Did you know that our country is ninety-nine years older than you?" she asked her little brother. He answered with one of his nonsense words, and Laura nuzzled the top of his downy head.

In June, the grasshoppers did come back. Once more, they ate every last grain of the Ingalls family's crop. They ate every green thing from horizon to horizon.

Instead of the glorious celebration of one hundred years of independence that Laura had looked forward to, July 1876 was a strange, worried time. Besides the grasshopper plague, there was bad news from the West about the Indian wars. On June 25, the Sioux and Cheyenne had wiped out General Custer and his troops at the Battle of Little Bighorn.

One night Pa sat at the table after dinner, drinking his tea in silence. Finally he said,

"I won't stay in such a blasted country."

"*Charles,*" said Ma. *Blasted* was almost a swear word, and Mary and Laura and Carrie were listening.

Pa went on: "A lot of folks are leaving. William Steadman told me *he* wouldn't stay another season. The Steadmans are buying a hotel in Burr Oak, Iowa, this fall. Steadman asked if we might go in with them and help run the hotel."

So it was settled: The Ingalls family would leave Plum Creek. Pa sold the farm, and they left for eastern Minnesota. They would stay with Uncle Peter and Aunt Eliza on the Zumbro River for the harvest season, until it was time to join the Steadmans in Burr Oak.

Packing their belongings into the covered wagon again, the Ingallses headed east. Laura knew that Pa wished they were heading west, and so did she. She was sorry to leave the creek, with its fishing holes and wading pools, and the little mesa up on the prairie where the girls had pretended to hold a fort against attacking Indians.

Never mind—it was jolly to be on the road again. The first day, Pa began to whistle as he drove the wagon. When they stopped for lunch, Ma insisted on combing the girls' hair before they ate. There was no one around to see their wild hair, but that didn't matter to Ma. She combed and braided Mary's golden hair, and Laura's brown hair, and Carrie's brown hair. "Nice girls have their hair combed sometime in the morning, at least," she said.

"Aren't you going to comb and braid Freddie's hair, too?" Pa teased her. They all laughed, and Ma ran the comb lightly over the baby's head, fuzzy like a peach.

After days of traveling through bare, dusty, grasshopper-eaten prairie, they came to the grassy pastures and the grain-filled fields of eastern Minnesota. Before long, the covered wagon pulled up to the door of Uncle Peter and Aunt Eliza's farmhouse. Cousins Alice, Peter, Ella, and Lansford came running to greet them. So did Edith, no longer a baby.

There was plenty of work on the farm for the older children, but the work here, shared with the cousins, was almost like play. The wild plums near the river ripened, and the cousins spent hours wandering through the plum thickets, eating and picking. They drove the cows out to pasture in the morning and drove them back late in the afternoon. Laura loved to feel the grass, soft under her bare feet, to watch the light and shadow flickering on the river and the reflection of trees and flowers in quiet pools, to listen to the tinkle of cowbells.

At the end of August, these carefree times came to an end. Baby Freddie got a fever. The top of his head felt hot to Laura's touch, and he made fretful noises even when Ma was holding him. When Laura saw the doctor ride up with his black bag fastened to his saddle, she drew a deep breath of relief. A doctor had cured Ma when she was so sick, and now surely this doctor would make Freddie get well.

But Freddie's fever kept burning, and he whimpered as he clenched up his body. A few days later, on August 27, the baby straightened out his body one last time—and he was dead. Laura could not believe it, but it was true.

Ma and Pa had always tried to make the best of things. "All's well that ends well," they'd say. Or, "There's no great ill without some small good." But they didn't say anything like that about Freddie's death. Neither did Uncle Peter or Aunt Eliza. Ma wrote a new entry in the family Bible, under "Deaths."

The next several weeks passed in a kind of grayness. The fall rains began, so that the sky was always gray. And the whole Ingalls family seemed to feel gray inside, too, with a heavy sadness.

Finally it was time to load the wagon, leave Uncle Peter's, and drive south to Burr Oak, Iowa. Pa sat on the wagon seat with cold rain running off his hat and shoulders. The cover over the wagon kept most of the rain off Ma and the girls, but still their clothes and the bedding were clammy. And worse, they did not leave behind the heavy sadness from Freddie's death. It traveled with them.

Burr Oak was quite a town, in Laura's eyes. It wasn't a new town, like Walnut Grove, but an old one with brick buildings as well as wooden ones. There were *two* hotels.

The hotel the Steadmans had bought, the Burr Oak House, seemed grand to Laura and Mary. On the main floor alone there were a barroom (of course children weren't allowed in there), an office, a parlor, and a parlor bedroom for the most important guest. That was Mr. Bisbee. He owned several properties in Burr Oak, but he lived in the hotel.

Downhill behind the main floor were the kitchen and the dining room. Mrs. Steadman pointed out holes in the door of the dining room. "Bullets," she said. Ma signaled to her not to talk about it in front of the girls.

Later, Laura and Mary got the whole thrilling story from Amy, the hired girl. The bullets, Amy explained, had been fired by Will Masters, the son of the man who used to own the hotel. He had chased his wife, Nannie, through the hotel one night, waving a pistol. "She slammed the door in his face, she did! And he fired right through the door!"

That winter, Laura and Mary helped with the work of the hotel. They made beds, washed dishes, and waited on tables. They also helped Mrs. Steadman by taking care of her youngest boy, Tommy. Ma would have expected them to do it, anyway, but Mrs. Steadman promised them "something very nice" for Christmas.

The promise of a reward made it easier to put up with Tommy, a whiny child. Laura couldn't help remembering how sweet and cheerful Freddie had been. Of course, Mrs. Steadman was always slapping and shaking Tommy, which would make anyone whine.

To tell the truth, Laura didn't like any of the three Steadman boys. Ma told her and Mary to be especially kind to Johnny Steadman, a boy about Mary's age. He had one leg shorter than the other and walked with a limp. But Johnny liked to pinch the girls, pull their braids, and tear their books, knowing they weren't allowed to fight back. Reuben Steadman, the middle brother, wasn't much better. In bed at night, Mary and Laura would whisper about how much they missed their cousins.

Sometimes Laura sang to Tommy, trying to cheer him up. Mr. Bisbee heard her, and took a notion to give her singing lessons. "Must I, Ma?" asked Laura. "I already know how to sing."

"It would be rude to say no," said Ma. "Mr.

Bisbee has studied music, and it's kind of him to give you the benefit of his education." So Laura had to stand beside the piano in the parlor and sing scales: "Do, re, mi . . ." while Mr. Bisbee counted time. Johnny peeked in the door and made faces, but Laura pretended not to notice.

Christmas of 1876 was the only dreary Christmas that Laura could remember. Pa and Ma seemed tired and busy all the time. Mrs. Steadman did not give Mary and Laura anything, in spite of what she had promised. As usual, Pa and Ma provided candy and little presents for the girls' stockings, and Laura and Mary and Carrie made gifts for their parents and one another. But no one felt like celebrating.

Fire!

Early in 1877, Pa and Ma decided to get out of the hotel business. The Ingallses were all glad to move out of the hotel and settle into rooms above a grocery store on Main Street. Pa ran a gristmill—farmers brought him their corn and wheat, and he ground it into meal or flour with a millstone turned by his team of horses. Ma kept house, and Mary and Laura went to the redbrick schoolhouse two blocks away, up on a hill.

Mary turned twelve that January, and she gasped with delight when she opened her birthday present from Pa and Ma. So did Laura, looking over Mary's shoulder. *"The Independent Fifth Reader!"* exclaimed Laura. The book was like a treasure chest, overflowing with stories and poems and speeches. The reader was almost like a present for Laura, too, because of course Mary would share it with her.

The girls liked their young teacher, Mr. Reed. His specialty was elocution, or public speaking, and he trained his students in how to use their voices. In the evenings, Laura and Mary would practice reading aloud from *The Independent Fifth Reader* for their parents and sisters. They read poems like "Paul Revere's Ride"; "The Village Blacksmith"; and "The Pied Piper."

Not all the students liked Mr. Reed. There was an older boy named Mose, who was bigger than Mr. Reed, who didn't even try to learn his lessons. Half the time he and his friends didn't come to school. Laura heard them bragging to the idle men who hung around outside the saloon that they were going to chase the teacher out of town.

One morning after school had begun, Mose swaggered in the door. His friends came in behind him, grinning. Laura felt sick with fear.

But Mr. Reed, at the front of the room, didn't look worried. "You are late, Mose," he said, tapping his heavy wooden ruler on the palm of his hand. "Come here."

This was exactly what Mose wanted, and he swaggered up the aisle. But just as he reached Mr. Reed, the teacher grabbed him by the collar and tripped him with his foot. Before Mose knew it, he was sprawled across the teacher's knees, being spanked like a bad little boy.

The students burst out laughing, even Mose's friends. When the teacher let him go, Mose slunk out of the school and never came back.

The Ingalls family liked their new home over the grocery store. The front room, with two windows looking out on Main Street, was sunny and comfortable. But unfortunately, the store was right next to the saloon. The girls tried to avoid walking past the front of the saloon, where rough-looking men hung around.

One night Ma woke up the girls in the middle of the night. "Mary. Laura. Get up and get dressed. The saloon is on fire. We must be ready to leave if the fire spreads to the store."

Throwing on her clothes, Laura ran into the front room and peered out the window. "Mary, there's Pa! Oh, and there's Mr. Bisbee."

The blazing saloon shed an eerie, quivering light on the town pump in the middle of the street. Pa and the rest of the men in town were lined up at the pump. One by one they filled buckets with water and threw it on the fire.

Mary leaned on the windowsill next to

Laura. "Look, the line has stopped. Why isn't it moving?"

"It's Mr. Bisbee," said Laura. "How can he take so long to fill his bucket? He's not even looking at it; he's just shouting." Then two other men pulled Mr. Bisbee away from the pump, and the fire-fighters' line moved forward again.

In the end, the fire was put out. Pa came home before dawn, looking tired, his face smudged with smoke. "Bisbee lost his head," he explained. "His bucket didn't have any bottom, and the water just poured through onto the ground, but he didn't notice. He kept shouting, 'Fire! Fire!' like a fool."

Ma set out a basin of warm water so Pa could wash up. "Well, at least no one was hurt," she said. "And our building wasn't touched. All's well that ends well."

"Yes," said Pa, "but if the darned saloon could have burned up without burning the town, I wouldn't have carried a drop of water."

"I guess Mrs. Cameron would have been glad of that," said Ma quietly. The Camerons were the couple who ran the grocery store below. Mr. Cameron was often in the saloon, leaving his wife to run the store.

One night sometime later, Pa discovered Mr. Cameron quarreling with his wife and drunkenly carrying a lamp dripping kerosene around his house. That was too dangerous, and the Ingalls family decided to move again. They rented, from Mr. Bisbee, a little brick house, near the oak woods on the edge of town.

It was springtime now, and Laura was glad to live in a place where they could keep a cow. Mary preferred to stay indoors, quiet and clean, but Laura loved to lead the cow out to the pasture in the early mornings and evenings. She walked barefoot through bright green grass and buttercups and dandelions. A brook, edged with wild iris, ran through the pasture.

Toward the end of May, a new Ingalls baby

was born: Grace Pearl. The baby was as beautiful as a spring flower, Laura thought. She had golden hair like Mary's and. bright blue eyes like Pa's.

Pa was delighted with little Grace, too, but Laura could see that he wasn't content these days. The gristmill season was over, so he was working for farmers as a day laborer. He didn't make much money, and he had to be away from home most of the time.

We don't own this house we live in, thought Laura. We don't own any land. The summer was over, the Ingallses had been in Burr Oak for almost a year, and they didn't seem to be any better off than when they'd left Walnut Grove, Minnesota. Except for Baby Grace, of course.

On the evenings when Pa was at home, he played restless, longing music on his fiddle: "My Old Kentucky Home" and "There Is a Happy Land (Far, Far Away)." And he would finish with a march, like "When Johnny

Comes Marching Home," as if his feet were itching to be moving forward.

Laura wasn't surprised when Pa began talking, one evening at suppertime, about moving west again. The trouble was, they had debts in Burr Oak. If they paid the grocer and Dr. Starr and Mr. Bisbee, the landlord, they wouldn't have enough money for the journey back to Walnut Grove.

"I asked Bisbee if he couldn't wait for the rent. I'd send it to him as soon as we got settled," said Pa. His voice rose with anger. "He said if we tried to leave without paying, he'd seize our horses!"

"Charles," said Ma, meaning for him to speak quietly. She added, "Shame on him for doubting your word."

Pa lowered his voice, but he still sounded angry. "I've always paid what I owed. Now I'll pay Dr. Starr and the grocer, but I'll be darned if I ever pay that rich old skinflint Bisbee a cent."

Laura was shocked at first—Pa, planning not to pay a debt? Her father was the most honest man she had ever known. But Mr. Bisbee had insulted him terribly, treating him as if he couldn't be trusted. Mr. Bisbee deserved to be cheated.

A few nights later, Ma shook the girls awake out of a sound sleep. Outside the door of the brick house the wagon waited, the canvas cover stretched over its top. Everything was loaded except the girls' bed. In the dark and quiet, Pa hitched the horses to the wagon and hoisted the bed in—and off they drove.

Laura didn't make a peep, but inside she was thrilled. She wanted to jump up and down and shout. Rich, mean Mr. Bisbee could *not* tell Pa what to do! The Ingalls family were on their way again, toward better times.

By daybreak they were in Minnesota, out of reach of the Burr Oak, Iowa, sheriff. The sun rose in a burst of color, as if to celebrate with them. After a stop for breakfast and to let the horses graze, Pa turned the wagon west. They were going to try their luck in Walnut Grove again, because the grasshopper plague was over.

They were all happy to be out in the fresh September air. In the evenings by the campfire, Pa played merry songs: "Yankee Doodle," and "Buffalo Gals," and "Arkansas Traveler." He seemed happier than Laura had seen him in a long time.

A Proposal of Marriage

When the Ingalls family drove their covered wagon into Walnut Grove in the fall of 1877, they got a hearty welcome from their friends. The Ensign family took them in and urged them to stay for the winter. Charles could earn good money working as a carpenter for Mr. William Masters, who owned a hotel and a great deal of the land in town. Mary, Laura, and Carrie could walk to school with their old friends, Anna and Howard Ensign.

Howard and Laura were both ten. Laura liked Howard, and she could tell that he liked her even more. Sometimes she caught him gazing at her with an adoring expression.

One morning after the first snowfall, as they followed Mary and Anna to school, Howard pulled Laura's hand to get her to fall back with him. In a soft voice he asked, "Laura . . . will you marry me?"

Laura was surprised, but pleased. She knew it was quite a compliment to be asked to marry someone. "We're too young to get married," she said.

"I mean, when we grow up," said Howard in the same soft voice. "Will you promise to marry me, Laura? Oh, please, say yes!"

Laura looked at Howard's eyes, large and brown like a dog's, and she didn't want to disappoint him. "I can't answer right away. I have to think it over."

"But you will think it over seriously, won't you, Laura?"

"Yes," said Laura. "I will."

The next morning, two other children,

Albert Moses and his sister, joined Laura and Howard on the way to school. They had a lovely snowball fight, with Laura and Albert exchanging the fastest volleys and laughing until they fell down.

At recess that day, Howard pulled Laura aside. "How could you, Laura?" His voice caught on a sob. "How *could* you play with another boy? We are going to be married!"

Disgusted, Laura looked away from the tears in his eyes. "I only said I would think it over," she snapped. "And the answer is *no!*"

The following spring, 1878, Charles Ingalls bought a piece of land, part of the pasture behind the Masters Hotel. He built a new house, and the family moved in before it was even finished. The Ensigns were good friends, but the Ingallses were happy to have a home to themselves again. "In our own house, it doesn't matter if Grace cries a bit in the night," said Ma. Pa opened a butcher shop in Walnut Grove and did a decent business, since families had run out of their home-butchered meat by this time of the year.

Laura was eleven now, and she noticed that things seemed different at school. The girls had divided into groups. There was the group of older girls, including Anna Ensign and Mary. There were the younger girls, like Carrie.

In the group of girls Laura's age there were two she didn't like: her old enemy, Nellie Owens, and Genevieve Masters. Genevieve's father, Samuel Masters, had just moved his family to Walnut Grove. He was the brother of William Masters, who owned the hotel.

Nellie was as stuck-up and spoiled as ever. Genevieve was even more stuck-up—she was always talking about how refined folks were in New York, where she came from. She wore the most elegant dresses to school, and she spoke with an affected lisp.

Luckily Nellie and Genevieve were rivals, always trying to bribe the other girls with candy or favors to side with one of them or the other. But as the spring went on, the girls Laura's age didn't follow either Nellie or Genevieve. Instead, they began following Laura.

Although Laura didn't give any bribes, she was a lot of fun. She led the girls to join in the boys' games, in spite of disapproving looks from her sister Mary. "They're calling you a *tomboy*," she warned.

"I don't care," said Laura. She was proud that she was the second fastest runner in the whole school. Because of her, the boys let the girls play baseball with them.

Laura was proud that she did well in her lessons, too. Thanks to Mr. Reed's training in Burr Oak, she liked to read out loud in school. She didn't even mind standing up in front of the school to give answers, because she knew she spoke well.

After school ended for the summer, Laura went to work at the Masters Hotel. Her pay was good money: fifty cents a week. And the work wasn't too hard: washing dishes, waiting on tables, and taking care of the Masters' baby granddaughter. Laura felt such a shivery chill when she first saw the baby's father. He was the same man who had fired the bullets through the dining room door in the Burr Oak House!

While Baby Nan was sleeping, Laura was allowed to read Mrs. Masters's *New York Ledger* papers. The papers had the most exciting stories about jewels and secret caverns, about people falling helplessly in love and getting into terrible dangers and then somehow getting out again. There were also things going on, right at the Masters Hotel, as interesting as the stories in the papers.

For instance, Mr. and Mrs. Masters had a spoiled older daughter, Mattie. She had the parlor bedroom, with its fine, snowy bed linen and silk draperies, although this room ought to have been given to the most important guest in the hotel. Mrs. Masters and

Nannie and Lotie, a poor cousin who lived with the Masterses, rose early every morning and worked hard all day. But Matie, instead of working, spent her time dressing up and flirting with Dr. Hoyt.

Dr. Hoyt, the young doctor who boarded at the hotel, had been engaged to Fanny, the daughter of a doctor in Burr Oak. Matie and Fanny had also known each other in Burr Oak, and they were supposed to be friends. But as Laura watched and listened from the sidelines, Matie got Dr. Hoyt to fall in love with her—and finally to marry her. It was just the kind of story of romance and passion and treachery that Laura found in Mrs. Masters's newspapers.

There were many fascinating stories in real life, Laura was discovering. In March 1879, Charles Ingalls was elected justice of the peace for Walnut Grove. He heard cases right in his front room, and the Ingalls girls listened to them eagerly from behind the kitchen door. It was shocking (but so interesting!) what some people would do to one another, even to friends—even to family.

The worst case Laura heard was brought by a Mrs. Welch, who took a terrible revenge on her own *sister*. Years ago the sister, a Mrs. Ray, had married the man Mrs. Welch had wanted. Mrs. Welch had held a grudge ever since, and now she was cheating her sister and brother-in-law out of their farm.

Laura listened to Mrs. Ray sobbing as the legal description of the property was read. Laura could imagine, just from hearing the simple facts about the property, what a beautiful place that farm must be. How awful for Mr. and Mrs. Ray to lose their farm—their home, and their means of making a living.

What if Mary hated Laura the way Mrs. Welch hated Mrs. Ray? Laura shuddered. She was beginning to understand why Ma and Pa had always been so strict with their daughters about not fighting. Even as little girls, Laura and Mary had never been allowed to hit each other. They weren't allowed to quarrel, either—or even to criticize each other. Maybe Mrs. Welch hadn't been taught to get along with her sister, and so finally she had ended up hating her.

Laura felt thankful that she and Mary knew how to get along. Mary could be annoying at times, but she was Laura's dear sister. Laura couldn't imagine how a husband, no matter how wonderful, could ever mean more to her than Mary did.

Mary's Eyes

"Why are you holding your head, Mary?" asked Laura.

It was a spring morning in 1879. Laura was clearing the breakfast dishes from the table while Mary swept the kitchen floor. Mary had paused with her hand to her forehead. "Just a little headache," said Mary, and she started to sweep again. Then she groaned and put both hands to her head, letting the broom clatter to the floor.

"Ma!" called Laura, frightened. Their

mother had already heard Mary, and she came running into the kitchen.

Ma put Mary to bed, but her headache grew worse. And she was burning with fever. Over and over Laura put cool, wet cloths on her sister's forehead, and in a short while the cloths would be warm from Mary's skin. She muttered and babbled, out of her mind with the fever.

To keep Mary's head cooler, Ma cut off her long golden hair. Laura remembered how she and Mary had quarreled, when they were little, about who had the prettiest hair. Now, it hurt Laura to look at Mary's stubbly scalp.

Mary lay sick in bed for several days. One morning, Laura was shocked to notice that her sister's face was pulled out of shape on one side. "She's had a stroke," said Ma, her usually calm voice trembling. Into Laura's horrified mind came a picture of the two oak trees in front of the house in the Big Woods of Wisconsin. She remembered so clearly

Mary's tree, struck by lightning and disfigured on one side.

At last Mary's fever went down. To Laura's relief, Mary's face smoothed out, and she began to get out of bed during the day to sit in the rocker. But Mary couldn't see as well as before, and the better she felt, the worse her eyes got.

The doctors said that the stroke had damaged the nerves to Mary's eyes, and there was no cure. Finally there came a day when Mary could barely see Grace's bright blue eyes. The next day, she saw nothing at all.

The whole family was stunned. All around Walnut grove the prairie was beautiful with new grass and wildflowers, but to Laura it looked as bleak as in December. It still seemed bleak, the day that Pa's younger sister Aunt Docia Forbes drove up to the door.

The Ingallses hadn't seen Docia since they'd lived in the Big Woods of Wisconsin.

Aunt Docia was on her way west to join Uncle Hiram. He was already in the Dakota Territory, running a railroad camp for the Chicago and North Western Railroad.

Pa had been looking tired and beaten lately, but now he sat up straight, and his eyes sparkled like blue glass. "If I work for the railroad for a season, that would give me money to stake out a homestead claim in the Dakota Territory. One hundred and sixty acres of free land, the government will give us!"

Laura felt her spirits lighten, and the other faces around the supper table looked hopeful, too. Only Ma looked worried. "Move *again*, Charles?"

Pa gave her an understanding look. "This will be our last move, Caroline, I promise. We'll settle down. The girls will have a good education."

"If we can make a go of homesteading," said Ma slowly. "We have to put up a house, and improve the land before five years are up." But now hope sparkled in her eyes, too.

The next day Pa had to sell their house in Walnut Grove and leave quickly, because Uncle Hiram needed him right away. Ma and the girls would stay behind, for now, to let Mary get her strength back.

Before Pa left, Laura went out to keep him company while he hitched the horses to the wagon. "You must be Mary's eyes for her now, Half-Pint," he told her. "Do you understand what I mean?"

Laura felt serious. "You mean, I must describe things for Mary so that she can see them in her mind." It was as if she were taking Mary's place as the oldest girl in the family.

In the days after Pa left, at first Mary couldn't do much except hold Grace on her lap. Then little by little Mary began to discover how much she could still do, even though she couldn't see. Before Laura could say, "Ma's coming in the door," Mary would recognize their mother's footsteps. When Laura or Ma brought in vegetables from the garden, Mary could wash and peel them by touch. Laura and Carrie became very careful to put every pan and spoon and towel back in its proper place, so that Mary could find them.

By summertime, Mary felt strong enough to go for walks with Laura. One evening, as the sun was going down, they strolled out on the prairie. "Birds are flying against the sunset," Laura told Mary. Those words didn't seem exact enough to let Mary "see," and she tried again. "Swallows are swooping low over the grass, very fast. Just one hawk is floating high above. They all look black against the gold sky and the streaks of rose-pink clouds."

"I can see it all in my mind," said Mary. Laura was happy—she was helping Mary, and doing what Pa had asked her to. The surprising thing was that Laura seemed to see more clearly herself, describing the scene for Mary.

As the weeks went on, Mary learned to wash the dishes and cook and hang out the

laundry without seeing. At the same time, Laura learned how to paint pictures for her sister with words. Using words this way was a skill, thought Laura, like sewing—only much, much more fun.

By the end of the summer, Ma thought Mary was well enough to travel. Pa, out at the railroad camp, sent Ma his first paycheck. Then Ma, Laura, Mary, Carrie, and little Grace went to the railroad station to take the train west from Walnut Grove to Tracy.

As the train roared into the Walnut Grove station, Laura was so scared, she couldn't speak. It was pleasant to see a train from a distance as it rushed across a bridge. But to stand on the platform by the tracks, with the boards trembling under her feet, deafened by the screaming whistle as the iron monster bore down on them—that was something else.

The train stopped in front of them with a crash, as if it were falling apart. Black smoke poured from the smokestack, and bits of ash settled on their freshly washed and ironed dresses. Glancing at the others, Laura could see that Mary and even Ma were scared, too. Carrie, only eight and not very strong, looked as though she might faint. Only Grace, in Ma's arms, seemed to think she was safe.

But once they were sitting on their plush seats inside the railroad car, and the train had started to move, Laura wasn't afraid anymore. She was too thrilled, and too busy watching the other passengers and the scenery flying by outside the window.

"It looks as if the farms are rushing past us, instead of the other way around," she told Mary. "There goes a barn with haystacks! There goes a whole big wheat field, cut down to yellow stubble!" She was about to add, "Riding the train is like riding in a wagon with runaway horses." But then she decided not to, especially since little Carrie was listening.

Pa met them with the wagon at the railway station in Tracy. They drove out of town onto the empty prairie, over the Minnesota border into Dakota Territory. *West!* thought Laura, shading her eyes from the setting sun. For the Ingallses, the direction of happy changes was the West.

For their first few weeks in Dakota, the Ingalls family stayed at the railroad camp in Brookings. Then Uncle Hiram's crew finished that section of the railroad, and everyone moved camp farther west. The new site, on Silver Lake, would soon be a town called De Smet.

Pa and Ma didn't allow the girls to go near the rough men in the railroad crew, but every day Pa brought home news. One evening he came home to supper laughing, with a story about the new supervisor, a city slicker from the East. The supervisor's job was to ride up and down the railroad line, spying on the crews for the railroad and docking the workers' pay if they were a few minutes late. All the men hated him. There'd been grumbling and slacking, Pa said, since he'd first started.

Today the grading crew had been scraping dirt from a swell on the prairie, dumping it into wagons and hauling it to fill a low place. All this work would make a level bed for the track. The city slicker, wearing his white starched collar and tie and tailored suit, showed up just before noontime and rode down to the dump, where the wagons were being filled. As he was criticizing the work and telling the men how to do their jobs, Big Jerry—part Indian, part French—rode up on his white horse.

"Big Jerry listened for a minute without saying anything," Pa said. "Then he took hold of the city fellow's bridle and led him under the dump, between the wagons. Instead of going into a wagon, the next scraperful of dirt fell right on his head. So did the next, and the next. Somehow now his collar wasn't so white, and his nose wasn't so high in the air.

All the men roared, but Big Jerry didn't move an eyebrow."

Everyone at the supper table laughed, too. Laura laughed so hard, she almost dropped the plate of biscuits she was bringing to the table. It was just what the stuck-up, bossy supervisor deserved. It reminded Laura of the time she and Mary had led Nellie Owens into the mud and she'd come out with leeches all over her.

Laura thought it was jolly in the railroad camp. She made friends with Aunt Docia's daughter, Cousin Lena. The two girls had some wild times, riding horses bareback. They also milked the cows and drove them out to pasture and back, every morning and evening. Laura and Lena sang as they worked, so Laura learned new songs from Lena, and Lena from Laura.

Two of their favorite songs were "She Was Only a Bird in a Gilded Cage" and "Where, Oh Where, Has My Little Dog Gone?" They also sang "A Railroad Man for Me." "I wouldn't marry a farmer," this song began. "He's always in the dirt." Laura sang it softly so Ma and Pa wouldn't hear. She thought the song was funny, but it might hurt their feelings.

When cold weather set in, the railroad crews had to stop work for the winter, and they all left the site. But Pa and Ma decided to stay for the winter, living in the surveyors' roomy, well-stocked house. An oxen driver, Walter Ogden, boarded with the Ingallses. In the evenings, Pa whittled a checkerboard, and then he played checkers with Walter Ogden. Laura learned to play, too—so well that she could beat both of them.

Winter evenings were also times for music. Pa played the fiddle, and they sang all the old songs, and some new ones, like "Old Stubbins on the North-Western Line," that Pa had learned from the railroad men. He played hymns, too. His favorite was "In the Sweet Bye and Bye."

That was a mild winter, and in mid-February of 1880 the weather was clear enough for Charles Ingalls to walk forty miles east to the land office at Brookings. There he paid the $13.86 filing fee on a good piece of land he had found, a mile northeast of what would soon be the town of De Smet. Now the land rush was on, and men poured into the area to stake out their claims. For a few months there was nowhere for all the newcomers to stay.

To help the newcomers out, and to make a little money, the Ingallses turned the surveyors' house into a stopgap hotel. Every morning and every evening, the kitchen was full of hungry men. And every night, the first floor of the house was covered with men snoring, muttering—and *trying* to sleep.

The girls, in their beds upstairs, sometimes giggled at the men's remarks: "Who put the dead mouse in my blanket?" Or, "I can't find my pillow. Oh, here it is—in my ear."

Laura was just thirteen, but in some ways she felt much older these days. She pinned up her braids to get them out of the way as she swept and cooked and set food in front of the boarders. Since her own dresses were shabby now, and too short, she put on an extra dress of Mary's. It came down to her ankles. Suddenly, in long skirts and pinned-up hair, she was no longer a child. And she was doing a woman's work alongside Ma.

The Worst Winter

The Ingalls family hadn't liked running the hotel in Burr Oak, and they didn't much like running a hotel in their home, either. They were glad when a real hotel went up in De Smet. It was one of the first buildings in town, after the saloon and the grocery store.

Charles Ingalls bought two prime corner lots on Main Street. He put up store buildings, and the family moved into the one across from Fuller's hardware store. The store had a front room for Pa's business, and a back room for the family's kitchen, where they cooked and ate and sat around the stove in cold weather. The back entrance was through a lean-to, where Pa stored coal for the stove. Upstairs, over the store, were two bedrooms, one for Pa and Ma and one for the girls.

The town was full of people busily putting up stores and staking out claims like the Ingallses. One neighboring family was the Garlands, who started a boardinghouse. Mrs. Garland was a widow, and Cap Garland was Laura's age. Two other newcomers Pa met were the Wilder brothers, Royal and Almanzo, from Spring Valley, Minnesota. They and their sister Eliza had filed on claims just north of De Smet in the summer of 1879.

With the train running through De Smet, land around the town was valuable to farmers. The train would carry their crops to markets in the East. And settlers could gain ownership to a piece of the Dakota Territory just by claiming it, living on it, and working it. More and more people poured into De Smet to seize their chance for free land. Not all of them could afford the hotels, and they had to stay in shanties, or camp wherever they could find empty ground.

One of these families, the Hunts, camped in back of Charles Ingalls's store. The Ingallses got to know Mr. Hunt, an old railroad worker, his wife, their grown son, Jack, Jack's wife, and their baby. Jack Hunt had filed on a homestead south of town, built a shanty, and broken the sod. But while he was away for a few weeks, working on the railroad to make money, a claim jumper had moved onto his homestead. When Jack showed up again, the claim jumper shot and killed him.

It was a terrible thing. Laura and her family did all they could to comfort the Hunts. At the same time, they took it as a warning. Pa said grimly, "We're moving out to our claim before some lowdown, no-good . . ." He couldn't seem to find a word bad enough for that kind of man. "Before someone jumps it."

Laura felt very sorry for the Hunts, especially Jack Hunt's young wife. But she was glad to leave the crowded, muddy town and move onto their homestead, where spring was coming on. Soon violets were blooming in protected hollows, and in June the perfume of wild roses drifted across the fields.

That was a happy summer, in spite of the hard work. After breaking the sod for planting wheat next year, Charles Ingalls put in quick crops like lettuce and turnips. Laura noticed that Pa was thin and tired. She also noticed how careful he was not to take more than his share of the food. I can help that way, too, thought Laura. She followed Pa's example and ate raw turnips between meals when she was hungry.

That fall, 1880, the first blizzard struck in October. Charles Ingalls quickly moved his family back into town, where he was county commissioner and justice of the peace. Like most people in De Smet, Charles ran his business in the front of his building, and the family lived in the back room and the bedrooms upstairs. The Ingallses didn't really have room for guests, but a young man named George Masters begged Ma to let his wife, Maggie, and their baby stay with them. He was working for the railroad, and he wanted to be able to see his wife on his time off.

The Ingallses didn't care much for George, a nephew of William Masters, the hotel owner in Walnut Grove. But they felt sorry for Maggie, and they thought the couple would only stay for a few weeks. Meanwhile, the second blizzard struck in the middle of a school day. Although the school was only a few blocks away, Laura and Carrie were barely able to struggle home to safety through the blinding snow and wind. While the storm was still raging, Maggie Masters's baby was born. Laura couldn't run to fetch the doctor, but Cap Garland's mother and Ma were with Maggie to help.

As the weeks went on, blizzard after blizzard hit town. Often there could be no school during the week, no church on Sunday. In the deadly storms, it was dangerous even to visit neighbors next door or across the street. Food was scarce, because trains couldn't get through the snow-blocked cuts on the railroad line. Flour ran out, and the townspeople had to grind their seed wheat in coffee grinders to make bread. Coal ran out, and they had to twist hay into sticks for fuel. To give Pa a rest, Laura took her turn in the freezing lean-to, twisting hay to burn.

It would have been a cold, miserable winter, anyway, but it was worse for the Ingallses with George and Maggie Masters under their roof. Charles and Caroline had always lived by the code of the pioneers, and they had brought up their daughters to live the same way: Work hard. Share. Be cheerful, even if you don't feel cheerful. Don't complain.

But George Masters seemed to have no

idea of these rules. Each dark, cold morning, George lay in bed while Charles Ingalls got up to start the fire and feed the animals in the barn. George didn't get up until breakfast was ready.

At the table, George helped himself first, even before his wife, though she was feeding their young baby. He often stuffed potatoes into his mouth so quickly that he burned his tongue. "Potatoes do hold the heat!" he would complain.

Laura wished George would at least go out to Fuller's hardware store or the Wilder brothers' feed store, as Pa did. The men in town gathered around the stove in one place or the other, telling stories and playing checkers and singing to pass the time. But the other men didn't like George any better than Laura did, and he stayed away from them. Day after day he huddled as close to the Ingallses' stove as he could, complaining about the cold. Laura finally snapped at him.

"If it isn't warm enough to suit you, Mr. Masters, *you* can go twist some hay—I'm tired."

Maggie Masters was more cheerful than her husband, but just as selfish. The cows were only giving a little milk, because of the cold and the poor fodder. Ma divided the milk between young Grace and Maggie, who was feeding the baby. Laura knew this was only right. But she thought Maggie might have protested a little, and at least tried to share.

Maggie was lazy like George, sitting by the stove all day with her baby—as if that excused her from doing any work. Blind Mary helped grind wheat, and even Carrie took a turn, although she wasn't strong. But not Maggie.

One evening after the meager supper, Laura said sweetly, "Let me hold the baby for you, Mrs. Masters, while you wash the dishes." Ma gave Laura a frown—you were *never* rude to guests, no matter how unwelcome. Maggie looked surprised and embarrassed, but she didn't stir. Laura was glad she'd finally spoken up, anyway.

As the winter went on and on, Laura and her family felt like prisoners in a cold, dark dungeon. Their only escape was times of singing together, or reading out loud, or reciting the poetry that they knew by heart. Then Laura discovered an even better escape: writing. By the light of the one kerosene lamp in the kitchen, she scribbled a poem of her own on a scrap of paper:

> *We remember not the summer*
> *For it was long ago*
> *We remember not the summer*
> *In this whirling blinding snow*
> *I will leave this frozen region*
> *I will travel farther south*
> *If you say one word against it*
> *I will hit you in the mouth.*

Finished, Laura felt satisfied and cheerful. A laugh bubbled up in her throat, but she swallowed the laugh, because she didn't want to draw attention to this poem. Ma and Mary wouldn't approve of it. She tucked the scrap of paper into her workbag with her sewing. She would show it to her friend Mary Power—if ever the winter ended and she got to see Mary again!

Late in the winter, even wheat to grind became scarce. Finally Almanzo Wilder and Cap Garland made a dash, between blizzards, to a settler twelve miles from town. They bought his whole stock of seed grain and hauled it back to De Smet to feed the hungry town. The two young men were the heroes of that hard winter—the worst winter in many years.

The first train to reach De Smet that spring arrived on May 9. George and Maggie Masters finally left the Ingallses' house. And soon after, the Ingalls family moved out to their homestead, where the prairie was green with new grass and dotted with wildflowers. For Laura, it was heavenly to be outdoors, in the middle of 160 acres, with no one around except her father and mother and sisters.

Miss Laura Ingalls, Teacher

For some time, Pa and Ma had been talking about sending Mary away to school. Ma had been a teacher before she married, and until Mary became blind, she had her heart set on becoming a teacher, too. That was impossible now, but Mary still longed for a good education. There was a special college for the blind in Vinton, Iowa. The Ingallses were determined to send Mary there, if only they could scrape the money together.

That summer a chance came up for Laura to make money by working at Clayson's dry goods store, helping Mr. Clayson's mother-in-law sew shirts. Laura would have to live in town with strangers, and she would have to spend all day, every day, sewing. Laura hated to leave home, and she hated sewing. But the money—twenty-five cents a day—was too good to pass up.

Living with the Claysons, Laura was shocked by the way the family quarreled. Also, she thought Mrs. Clayson and her mother were very silly. First they got upset about rumors of a "Catholic conspiracy." Mrs. Clayson paced the room, wringing her hands and declaring that "they" would never take her Bible away from her.

Then a comet appeared in the sky, and Mrs. Clayson and her mother seemed to think the end of the world was coming. (By chance, something terrible did happen, in faraway Washington, D.C. A crazy man shot President Garfield, and the papers said the president might die.)

Sitting by the window of the dry goods store, Laura kept her mouth shut and sewed her buttonholes. But inside, she was laughing at the two women. She didn't believe there was any Catholic conspiracy, and she didn't believe the comet in the sky meant the end of the world. But if the world *was* going to end, then why worry about the Catholics taking over? These two women were as witless, in their way, as the drunken men who stumbled out of the saloon across the street.

At the end of the summer Laura came triumphantly home with her pay. "Oh, Laura!" said Mary. "Now I can go to college." Mary couldn't see to look directly into her sister's eyes, but the expression on her face thanked Laura better than anything.

Laura was happy for Mary, but at the same time, she was sad. What would life be like, without her older sister? She and Mary had played and worked and quarreled together and slept in the same bed, ever since Laura could remember.

To mark this important occasion, Mary's leaving home, Pa drove the three older girls into town and had a photographer take their picture. They had to hold absolutely still for the camera, so the picture wouldn't come out blurred. "Just pretend we've frozen stiff in the blizzards," said Laura.

Mary sat ladylike on a stool, her hands crossed in the lap of her new checked dress. Carrie stood at Mary's right, wearing the dress trimmed with plaid that used to be Laura's Sunday dress. Laura, at Mary's left, wore a checked dress like Mary's, with a ribbon pinned at her throat. She stood tall, as if she were reciting a poem in school.

Shortly afterward, Pa and Ma took Mary on the train to Vinton, Iowa. Mary would be away at school for years, only coming home during vacations. Things would never be the same.

❅ ❅ ❅ ❅

By the fall of 1881, De Smet had grown so much that there were many newcomers in the school. As always, Laura felt shy around strangers, and she was grateful to see her friend Mary Power. They both liked one of the new girls, Ida Brown, daughter of the minister of the Congregational church. But none of them cared for Genevieve Masters, who had just moved to town.

What bad luck, thought Laura, that Genevieve had followed her from Walnut Grove to De Smet! Genevieve was as stuck-up and affected as ever, but now she was also tall, slim, and pretty. She had a lovely complexion, and she dressed for school as though she were going to a party.

The teacher, Miss Eliza Wilder, was new that fall. She was the sister of Almanzo Wilder, the young man who had risked his life to bring grain to the starving town during the Hard Winter. Miss Wilder must have some of her brother's gumption, thought Laura, because she was homesteading on her own.

But Miss Wilder didn't have much idea about how to teach. She seemed to want to make friends with her students! She told them an embarrassing secret, something you should tell only your best friend. As a girl, she had gotten head lice, and the other school-children had taunted her by chanting, "Lazy, lousy, Liza Jane."

As Laura listened to the teacher, her heart sank. Now no one would respect Miss Wilder. She wouldn't be able to teach any-thing—and Laura wouldn't *learn* anything. She wrote a verse on her slate and showed it to Mary Power:

> *By gum I must leave the school*
> *For teacher looks like such a fool.*

Mary smothered a giggle, but Laura was immediately sorry. In the following days, she tried to keep the other children from teasing the teacher. But Miss Wilder had lost control completely. The school board did not rehire her for the winter term, and a sensible new teacher took over.

Laura, lively and cheerful, was more of a leader in school than ever. Laura might not be fashionably tall and slender like Genevieve Masters, but she had large, expressive dark blue eyes and thick, shiny brown hair. She still wasn't afraid of being called a tomboy, and she led the other girls to join in snowball fights and sled rides with the boys.

At the beginning of 1882, Laura was invited to her first party. That February, she turned fifteen. Now several boys were interested in Laura Ingalls. She was invited to more parties, and after revival meetings at church one young man or another would offer to escort her home. One of those young men was Almanzo Wilder.

At first, Laura was more interested in Cap Garland. She felt shy of Mr. Wilder (as she thought of him), ten years older than herself. And she had mixed feelings about boys in general. Some of them tried to kiss her, or put an arm around her shoulders when they were out for a buggy ride. She would not stand for that!

Another thing Laura felt stubborn about was corsets, the undergarment ladies wore to pinch in their waists. Before Mary had left for college, Ma insisted that Mary and Laura both start wearing corsets. "You are young ladies now," she said in her gentle but final tone. Mary wore her corset meekly, even at night. And Laura was sure she was still wearing it at college, hundreds of miles away from Ma.

But Laura rebelled. The steel stays laced tightly around her middle made her feel like a horse forced into a harness. She never wore her corset as much as her mother thought she should or laced it as tight as other girls did.

"Before I was married," Ma warned Laura,

"your father could span my waist with his two hands."

"Well, I don't want anyone's hands around my waist," answered Laura. She was surprised at herself, answering her mother back so pertly. But she truly thought her judgment about corsets, anyway, was as good as her mother's.

In school Laura made great strides in her lessons. If she studied hard, she could pass the examination for her teaching certificate when she was sixteen. Then she'd be able to earn enough money to keep Mary in college.

Before Laura was even sixteen, a nearby community offered her a two-month teaching job. She was doubtful that she could be a good teacher yet, and she was sure she didn't want to live away from home. But her family needed the money—so she said yes.

Laura's hosts in that school district were the Bouchie family. Laura tried to be pleasant with them, but Mrs. Bouchie wouldn't even talk to her. I wish I were back with the Claysons at the dry goods store, Laura thought as she lay in bed the first night. The Claysons were foolish and quarrelsome, but at least they didn't seem to want to kill anyone.

Mrs. Bouchie hated homesteading, and it made her hate everyone around her. Laura had heard about pioneer women like this. They got "the blues" from living out on claim shanties for years on end with only children for company. Sometimes they cried all the time, or talked to themselves, or turned hateful like Mrs. Bouchie.

But Laura did well at teaching, in spite of being homesick and anxious. She kept reminding herself how much her family needed the good pay she was making. And to her surprise and delight, she didn't have to spend weekends with the Bouchies. Every Friday afternoon Almanzo Wilder turned up, even in the worst winter weather, to drive her home.

It did make Laura a little nervous that

Almanzo was paying so much attention to her. He was a full-grown man with his own homestead claim and his own beautiful team of matched Morgan horses. She felt more comfortable with boys her age, like Cap Garland.

Laura also felt more comfortable being a student than a teacher, and she was glad to return to school in De Smet for the fall term of 1883. The school had a wonderful new teacher, Professor Owen. He expected a great deal of the students, and Laura found herself doing more than she could have imagined.

It was Professor Owen who had Laura write her first composition in school. "Ambition" was the subject he assigned the class. Laura doubted that she had anything to write about ambition. But reading the definition of the word in the dictionary, she thought, Why, ambition is what *I* have.

"Ambition is necessary to accomplishment,"

Laura began to write. She went on for two paragraphs, ending with a quotation from Shakespeare about ambition. Professor Owen, the teacher, praised her highly.

In her spare time at home, Laura had fun writing verses. Sometimes she stitched the handwritten pages together into little books. One of them began with a verse on its front cover:

> *When you open this book*
> *Just take one good look*
> *If the rhymes do not please*
> *You can close it with ease.*

Laura's booklet ended with a final verse on the back cover:

> *If you've read this book through*
> *With all its jingles*
> *I'll let you know that it's been filled,*
> *By Laura E. Ingalls.*

Laura in Love

Laura was proud to be seen behind Almanzo's team of fine Morgan horses, which he handled so well. As the seasons went by, he appeared at the Ingallses' farm nearly every Sunday afternoon. He took Laura for buggy rides in the warm weather and on sleigh rides in the winter.

Little by little Laura got more comfortable with Almanzo, until it seemed silly to call him "Mr. Wilder." She called him "Manly," because she didn't care for "Almanzo" or for his nicknames "Manzo" or "Mannie." He didn't much

like "Laura," either, and besides, he had a sister named Laura. So he called her "Bessie," a nickname for her middle name, Elizabeth.

Almanzo didn't talk much, but gradually Laura found out about his family and his life before he'd come to De Smet. He had been born in Malone, in upstate New York, and lived there until he was about sixteen. Then his family had moved to Spring Valley, Minnesota, twenty or thirty miles south of where Uncle Peter Ingalls and his family lived.

Besides his brother Royal and his sister Eliza, Almanzo had a younger brother and two other older sisters. The Wilders must be well-off, Laura guessed. Almanzo never bragged about how much his family owned, of course. But he would mention "the barns"—imagine having more than one barn!—or the "hired men." Pa had some-times been a hired man himself.

By the spring of 1884, Laura had gotten used to thinking of Almanzo as her "beau," or boyfriend. And then one Sunday afternoon she had an unpleasant surprise. When Almanzo picked her up for a ride, there was another girl in the buggy.

Laura knew this girl, Stella Gilbert. Laura thought the whole Gilbert family was shiftless. Some time ago, she'd refused to go to a party with Stella's brother.

At the end of the afternoon, Almanzo dropped Stella off at her family's farm. Driving away, he said to Laura, "I feel sorry for Stella. Her mother's bedridden, and she has to spend all her time taking care of her. I thought it would be nice for her to get out."

"I'm sure it *is* nice for her," said Laura. She felt ashamed of herself for begrudging Stella a buggy ride.

But as Stella appeared in Almanzo's buggy week after week, Laura stopped feeling sorry for her. She didn't like the way the other girl sat so close to Almanzo, or the flirty way she looked up at him from under her eyelashes. Laura suspected that Stella had more in mind than enjoying the scenery and fresh air.

Finally Laura decided that Almanzo would have to choose between her and Stella. When Almanzo pulled up his horses at the end of the ride that afternoon, Laura stepped down from the buggy without looking at him. "If you bring Stella along next Sunday," she said, "you needn't come for me." She hurried into the house, not waiting for his answer.

The next Sunday, only Almanzo was in the buggy behind his fine team of Morgans. "Good afternoon," said Laura sweetly as he handed her up into the buggy seat. She had won!

But as they drove off over the prairie, Laura began to cast sideways glances at Almanzo's calm profile. A suspicion popped into her head. Maybe he hadn't invited Stella along just to be kind. Maybe in his quiet way Almanzo had decided to test Laura's feelings, to make her think how sorry she'd be if some other girl nabbed him.

Well, Laura *didn't* want some other girl nabbing Almanzo. She turned away so he wouldn't see her blushing.

Laura had to admit she felt happy with Almanzo in a very special way. She felt comfortable being quiet with him as well as talking—they seemed to understand each other. Like Laura, Almanzo loved working with animals and living on the land. He had the same values that the Ingallses had always lived by: Work hard, don't complain, help your neighbor.

Ma and Pa thought well of Almanzo, too. Laura didn't realize *how* much her parents thought of Almanzo until the time she stayed out too late. Laura and Almanzo went to visit friends that evening, and they had so much fun that she lost track of the time.

Driving back to the Ingalls farm, Almanzo let his horses trot fast. But still it was past two o'clock by the time Laura crept into the dark house. This was much later than was proper for a young girl to be out alone with a man, and Laura expected a scolding the next day. But her parents didn't say a word.

Ma did ask, later, if Laura thought she was old enough to decide on a husband. "I was twenty when Charles and I were married, and still I was very young."

"I'm sure I know my mind, Ma." Laura couldn't explain why, but she was sure she would never have the kind of understanding with anyone else that she had with Almanzo. Sometimes, watching his pair of sleek Morgan horses, she thought that she and Almanzo were like his team. They were born to pull in harness together.

One evening in the summer of 1884, Almanzo brought a ring for Laura—a gold engagement ring set with a garnet and pearls. Even though Laura had already made up her mind to marry him, she felt breathless. As he slid the ring onto her finger, Laura couldn't speak.

By the next time Almanzo took her for a ride, though, her voice had returned, and even a bit of her sauciness. She held her left hand with the shining ring up to the sunlight and remarked, "You aren't the first to ask me, you know."

"What do you mean?" asked Almanzo.

"Why, when I was ten years old in Walnut Creek, Howard Ensign asked me to marry him. Only he cried when I played with another boy, and then I told him my answer was no."

Almanzo laughed. "Well, I'm glad you didn't marry Howard Ensign."

"So am I," said Laura in a suddenly soft voice.

Now that they were engaged, it was proper for Laura and Almanzo to be alone together in the evening. Ma and Pa would make a point of going to their bedroom at nine o'clock, so that the two young people could have the living room to themselves. It was understood that Almanzo was expected to leave by eleven o'clock. But one night, just before the clock struck eleven, he set it back an hour—and sat down on the sofa with Laura again. After Almanzo left, Laura reset the clock to the right hour.

That fall, Almanzo left with his brother Royal for Louisiana. They had both gained title to their homesteads in August, so they didn't need to live on their claims. They planned to drive a peddler's wagon all the way to a big fair in New Orleans. Then they would travel north to Spring Valley, Minnesota, to visit their parents, and they wouldn't return to De Smet until springtime.

So soon after Laura had decided to spend her life with Almanzo, she had to do without him for months! Of course she was busy with school—this was her last year—but there was a great gap in her life. She wrote a poem to express her feelings. It began,

> *Lonely! I am so lonely*
> *Far from thee.*
> *Days come and go,*
> *And are all the same*
> *To me.*

Almanzo didn't write poetry, or even say much about the way he felt. But he must have felt just the way Laura did, because he showed up at the Ingallses' door on Christmas Eve. They decided to get married the next fall, after the harvest was in.

Almanzo's older sister Eliza was visiting their parents in Spring Valley, Minnesota. She wrote Almanzo that she and their mother were planning a big church wedding for him and Laura in the fall. Almanzo had already told her they didn't *want* a big wedding, but Eliza and Angeline Wilder paid no attention.

Laura and Almanzo had planned to wait until after the busy harvest season to get married. But now it seemed more important to have the kind of wedding they wanted: small, quiet, and inexpensive. On August 25, 1885, Laura and Almanzo drove to the Reverend Brown's and were married in his parlor. The only witnesses were Mrs. Brown, Laura's friend Ida Brown, and Ida's fiancé.

The wedding ceremony was simple and traditional, except for one change in the vows: Laura did not promise to "obey" her husband. At that time, almost everyone assumed that the husband should be the head of the household. But Laura wanted her marriage to be an equal partnership—and so did Almanzo.

Rose and Rocky Ridge

"Yah-*hoo!*" screamed Laura, leaning forward in her saddle. It was a beautiful fall morning, so early that the sun hadn't melted the frost on the dry grass. Both Laura's pony, Trixy, and Almanzo's pony, Fly, bolted at her scream. "Race you to the shanty!" she called to Almanzo, with Trixy's thick mane whipping her face.

Laura and Trixy always won these races. She loved the pony Almanzo had bought for her, her small, quick feet and her large, responsive eyes.

When Almanzo caught up with Laura at the shanty, they were both laughing and breathless. "Do you think it's right for us to play so much?" asked Laura.

Almanzo knew she wasn't serious, but he said, "I should think so, after we've worked every day of the harvest season, before dawn until after dark."

"And after the crops were in," said Laura, "you broke the sod for a bigger wheat crop next year."

"And *you* didn't do much," Almanzo teased her, "except cook, clean, wash, iron, churn butter, preserve . . ."

Yes, she had done all that work, Laura thought with pride. The same endless work as at home, except she'd done it all herself without any help from her sisters or Ma.

It was the fall of 1885. The newlywed Wilders were young, healthy, and ambitious. They owned a homestead farm of 160 acres, to which Almanzo had gained title in 1884.

When they had "proved up" a tree claim of another 160 acres north of the homestead, they would own that land, too.

Almanzo had borrowed money to build their three-room house on the tree claim and to buy farm machinery, and Laura worried a little about being in debt. But a good harvest would more than pay off these debts.

As it turned out, the harvest of 1886 was ruined by a hailstorm. Instead of getting out of debt, the Wilders had to go further into debt with a mortgage on the homestead. But Laura didn't complain. She and Almanzo would work hard and pay off their debts. Meanwhile, they were going to have a baby. Laura was sure it would be a girl, and she knew what she wanted to name her: Rose, after the prairie roses Laura loved so much.

Laura and Almanzo's daughter, Rose, was born on December 5, 1886, in the middle of a snowstorm. Almanzo drove the sleigh to fetch Ma and then the doctor to help with the birth. After the baby was safely born, he drove the doctor back to town. Ma would stay a few days to take care of Laura.

Laura lay in bed with the baby in her arms. "A Rose in December," she murmured to the tiny bundle. In the lamplight the baby's features were delicate and perfect. "Isn't she a grand Christmas present, Ma?"

"She's a fine, healthy baby. Eight pounds." Ma smiled at Laura and little Rose. She added, "It was a snowy day when *you* were born, nineteen years ago."

For the first few weeks after Rose's birth, Laura was content to stay home, just resting and taking care of the baby. But by the middle of January, she was itching to go somewhere. "Let's drive out to see the folks," she said to Almanzo. "I'll wrap the baby up well."

The day was bitterly cold, but sunny. The sleigh runners squeaked on the dry snow, the sleigh bells jingled. All the wide expanse of the prairie was blank white, with only a few buildings at the edge of town showing on the horizon.

At the Ingallses' homestead, Ma and Pa scolded Laura for bringing little Rose out in the cold. But when Laura unwrapped the baby, they could see that Rose was fine, and they had to stop scolding and start admiring her. Ma sat in the rocker by the stove to hold Rose.

"Is that a smile?" cooed Ma, bending over the baby. "I must write Mary about that smile!"

"Look, Laura," said nine-year-old Grace. She was holding a notebook and a pencil. "I'm keeping a diary, and here's what I just wrote: '"January 12, 1887. Laura has a baby, and it is just beginning to smile.'"

Pa chuckled. "Everyone's writing about Miss Rose Wilder. Did you see the birth announcement in *The De Smet News and Leader?*" He unfolded a newspaper and read, "'The good angels called at the home of Mr. and Mrs. A. J. Wilder last Monday night, and left a bright little nine-pound girl to cheer their solitude. . . . Grandpa Ingalls is entitled to wear gray hairs and numerous wrinkles now.'"

Laura laughed. "I suspect Carrie wrote the last part." She was pleased to have her baby written about. In all the happiness of this time, it seemed good to have it put down in words on a page.

The year after Rose's birth, hard times hit. In the summer of 1887, the Wilders' barn burned down with all the grain and hay stored inside. The next year, Laura and Almanzo both got diphtheria and were dangerously ill for weeks. Laura recovered, but Almanzo was left with a permanent limp. A drought scorched the Midwest, and the crops failed year after year.

In 1889, Laura and Almanzo had a second child, a son. Sadly, the baby lived only two weeks. And shortly afterward, the Wilders' house caught fire and burned to the ground.

During the next few years, Laura and

Almanzo tried this and that in their struggle to make a bare living. They tried sheep farming instead of raising wheat; then they sold their homestead and traveled to Spring Valley, Minnesota, to stay with Almanzo's parents. Desperate, the young family even moved all the way to the Florida Panhandle and tried farming among the pine woods and swamps.

By the fall of 1892, the Wilders were back in De Smet, South Dakota, with no land and no money. The hot winds still blew over the prairie, and the dust storms choked the air. Laura and Almanzo longed for their own farm, but no farmer could make a living in South Dakota now. The Wilders needed a second chance—but where could they get it?

Then a neighbor in De Smet came back from a trip. He had been to Missouri, which the railroads were calling "the Land of the Big Red Apple." Sure enough, the apple he gave the Wilders was the biggest, reddest apple they had ever seen.

Just looking at that apple gave Laura new hope. "Maybe it's time to try a different kind of farming," she said to Almanzo. "Apple orchards."

In mid-July, 1894, the Wilders said good-bye to Ma and Pa, to Mary, Carrie, and Grace, and started out for Missouri. The horses' hooves raised clouds of dust as the Wilders drove east under a broiling sun. At the end of the first day they reached Yankton, South Dakota, on the Missouri River. They took a ferry across the river to Nebraska.

The Wilders traveled between drought-parched fields through Lincoln, Nebraska, and on into Kansas. Day after day, week after week, the wagon wheels rolled steadily southeast. Their goal was Mansfield, a small town in the Ozark Mountains on a railroad line. Since the Wilders planned to grow apples, they needed to be near the railroad, to ship the fruit to market.

At night in the campgrounds along the way, Laura took out her lap desk. It was precious to her, because Almanzo had made it for her. He had polished the wood silky-smooth and hinged it so that it unfolded into a slanted writing surface, lined with green felt. A lady with such a portable desk could always write, even sitting by a campfire on an upturned bucket.

The lap desk was also precious because the narrow tray at its top, with an inkwell and a groove for Laura's pen, hid a hundred-dollar bill. That hundred dollars was money Laura had scrimped and pinched to save. A hundred dollars, enough for a down payment on a piece of land, would buy them a new life in the hill country of Missouri.

Also precious to Laura, in another way, was the notebook and pencil in her lap desk. Every day she wrote about their journey in the little notebook, her diary.

We crossed the James River and in twenty

minutes we reached the top of the bluffs on the other side. We all stopped and looked back at the scene and I wished for an artist's hand or a poet's brain or even to be able to tell in good plain prose how beautiful it was. If I had been the Indians I would have scalped more white folks before I ever would have left it.

Week after week, the Wilders' wagon creaked and rattled onward. They passed through Topeka, Kansas, and crossed the state border near Liberal, Missouri. "I wonder, Manly," said Laura, "how far it is from here to Independence, Kansas."

"Less than a hundred miles, I'd say." Almanzo nodded toward the west. "Your pa had a claim there once, didn't he?"

"Yes. I don't remember it—I was too young—but the folks always told stories about that year on the high prairie."

A few miles farther on, the Wilders stopped

in Lamar, Missouri. Laura took Rose with her to the post office to mail letters back to De Smet. "This one is to Grandma and Grandpa," she told Rose, holding up a thick letter. "And this one is to Mr. Sherwood, the editor. Maybe he'll print the story of our trip in his newspaper."

"And Aunt Carrie will set the type to print our story, won't she, Mama?"

"Yes." Laura smiled at Rose, imagining Carrie working with *her* words at *The De Smet News and Leader* office.

From Lamar, the Wilders headed east toward Springfield. Soon the roads began to climb into the Ozark Mountains. As they jogged along, the climate turned cooler and the scenery prettier. "The wind," breathed Laura. "It's gone, that scorching prairie wind. . . . Manly, Rose—will you look at those apples!" She pulled a bright red one from a branch overhanging the road.

"Nobody planted that apple tree, the way

it's growing," remarked Almanzo. "Must be true, then, what they say." He meant that this part of the country was a good region for fruit farming. And so the Wilders could make a living by growing apples.

By plodding along at twenty miles a day for six weeks, the Wilders reached Mansfield at the end of August. They camped in a shady grove on the outskirts of town and began looking around for land to buy. A farm would cost about four hundred dollars. Laura and Almanzo had their one hundred dollars for a down payment, and a bank would lend them the rest.

After weeks of looking at different farms for sale, Laura and Almanzo found a place a mile outside of Mansfield. This forty-acre Ozark farm was just the opposite of the 320 acres of flat, fertile prairie they had left behind in South Dakota. "It's all hills," said Almanzo.

Gazing over the ridges running every

which way, Laura let out a long breath. Something about this place awoke her memories of another little farm on a ridge—in the Big Woods of Wisconsin.

"I wouldn't really call this place a *farm*," Almanzo went on. "Only four acres cleared and planted in apple trees. The rest is just brush, woods, and rocks."

"It'll be such a pretty place," said Laura.

Almanzo gave her an alarmed glance. "There's no house, just that one-room log cabin without any windows."

The cabin was an even rougher dwelling than the log cabin Pa had built on the Kansas prairie, but Laura wasn't going to admit that. "I've lived in log cabins before," she snapped. "If I can't have this land, I don't want any."

Laura didn't talk that way very often. But when she did, Almanzo always gave in. They bought the farm, and Laura named it Rocky Ridge.

* * * *

At last the Wilders were farmers again. Almanzo dragged his left foot as he walked—he would have that limp for the rest of his life. But even without his full strength he could do a hard day's work. He cleared out sassafras thickets, and little by little the space for orchards appeared.

Laura, as strong as ever, helped Almanzo cut down oak trees to haul into town and sell for firewood. "I'd rather have you at the other end of a cross-cut saw," he told her, "than any man I ever sawed with."

They were always tired at the end of the day, but Laura found time to write the folks back in South Dakota. She didn't know which she liked better, writing letters or getting them. One day, as Laura and Rose were gathering the fresh-smelling laundry from the clothesline, Almanzo returned from the post office in town with a letter from Ma. Laura dropped the last clothespins into the clothespin bag and stopped to open the letter.

"Oh, look," said Laura, "Ma sent a clipping from *The De Smet News and Leader*." Then she read the first words of the article, and she blushed with pleasure. *"Oh."* It was Laura's description of their trip from De Smet to Missouri. Those were her own words on the printed page, words that everyone in De Smet must have read by now.

There was laundry to fold, and then supper to cook, so Laura only ran her eyes quickly over the newspaper story. But that evening, when she sat down at the table with her knitting, she unfolded the clipping again. By the light of the kerosene lamp, knitting at the same time, she read the article aloud to Almanzo and Rose. "'We have had a very pleasant trip so far. . . . It is a continual picnic for the children to wade in creeks and play in the woods, and sometimes we think we are children and do likewise. We have eaten apples, grapes, plums, and melons until we actually do not care for any

more, and to satisfy a Dakota appetite for such things is truly something wonderful.'"

As Laura read on, Rose played on the floor, building her own little cabin from corncobs. Almanzo sat near the fire, oiling harnesses to keep the leather supple. Every now and then Laura looked over at their faces, which reflected the same glow she felt. A bit of their lives was now a story in print.

Writing from Life

During the next five years, Laura and Almanzo worked hard to turn Rocky Ridge into a paying farm. Slowly an apple orchard appeared, and a barn and pasture for cows, and a henhouse and a flock of chickens. Their home grew from a windowless log cabin into a two-room house with a loft for Rose. Rose started classes at the brick schoolhouse in Mansfield, where she was by far the brightest student.

With all the Wilders' hard work, it was a struggle to make a living. The whole country was still suffering through a depression. In

1897, Laura and Almanzo rented a small yellow house in town. There, Almanzo earned money by hauling goods from the train station in his wagon. Laura ran a boarding table in their home, serving meals to paying guests. But their hearts were at Rocky Ridge Farm.

The next year Laura and Almanzo had a visit—and a generous gift—from Almanzo's parents. The older Wilders bought the yellow house in town and gave it to their son and daughter-in-law. Now Laura and Almanzo wouldn't have to pay rent. They could use their money to pay off the mortgage on the farm and buy more farmland. Almanzo's dairy herd flourished, and so did Laura's flock of leghorn hens. The apple orchard began to bear boxcarloads of high-quality fruit.

In the fall of 1901, Laura had bad news from home: Pa was ailing with heart disease. By the spring of 1902, Pa was dying. Laura took the train from Missouri to South Dakota to see her father one more time.

In De Smet, Carrie picked Laura up at the train station in the buggy. "Oh, Laura, I'm so glad you're home," said Carrie as they drove to the Ingallses' house on Third Street. "It will do wonders for Pa." She gave her older sister a worried glance. "You mustn't expect— Pa doesn't have much color."

Inside, Laura found Pa in the downstairs bedroom. She understood why Carrie had tried to warn her, because his face was almost the same color as his gray beard. Worse, he was lying propped with pillows, instead of plowing a field or hammering a roof. "Pa!" She gave him a hug.

"Half-Pint," he murmured. And he added, like Carrie, "I'm glad you're home."

Laura stayed for weeks, sleeping in the guest room upstairs. During the day, she spent hours at Pa's side, reading aloud or telling him funny stories or just keeping watch. In the parlor, Mary played the organ to cheer them all up. Laura longed for the music of her father's fiddle—but Charles Ingalls would never play the fiddle again.

One Sunday afternoon early in June, Pa died. At his funeral in the Congregational church on Tuesday, they all sang "In the Sweet Bye and Bye," Pa's favorite hymn. Laura and Ma, Mary, Carrie, and Grace sang it out bravely, as they knew Pa would want them to.

The church was full of Charles Ingalls's friends. The whole town of De Smet, it seemed, had been his friends. At the burial in the cemetery, it was the wild roses that finally made Laura break down. Their sweet scent seemed unbearably sad to her, and their brilliant pink and red blurred in her tear-filled eyes.

On the long train ride home, Laura reread the death notice from *The De Smet News and Leader*. Mr. C. P. Ingalls had been the first to build a dwelling in De Smet, the newspaper said. The first religious services were held in his home, and he had helped found the Congregational church. "As a citizen he was held in high esteem . . . ," wrote the editor. "As a friend and neighbor he was always kind and courteous . . ."

Laura supposed this was high praise—but it seemed woefully lacking to her. She tucked the newspaper back into her carpetbag. Almanzo would enjoy reading *The Leader*, with all the news of people they used to know, and the crop reports.

Gazing out the window at the wheat fields flying past, Laura felt a fierce longing. Someone should write the *whole* story of Charles Ingalls, so that everyone would know what a splendid man Pa had been. His story would also be the story of this land when it was wild prairie, when Pa had driven his covered wagon across it at the rate of twenty miles a day.

Someone, sometime, should write that story, because it had all changed so much and so fast. The pioneer way of life was vanishing. It was an important part of American history, and it must not be forgotten.

Back in Mansfield, the feeling kept nagging at Laura. The next year, 1903, she tried to write some stories from her childhood. But there were always dishes to be washed, or the chickens to be fed, or socks to be darned. She didn't get very far.

For some time Laura and Almanzo had been worried about Rose's education. The Mansfield public school didn't even offer a high school degree, and the Wilders couldn't afford to send Rose to a private academy. In the summer of 1903, Almanzo's sister, Eliza, offered to take Rose to live with her in Crowley, Louisiana, to finish her schooling. The next June, Rose graduated from high school in Louisiana with honors.

When Rose returned home to Mansfield that summer, she was more restless than before. Rose had the skills and strength for farmwork, thought Laura—she could milk cows, ride and drive horses, cook and sew. But Rose didn't want to spend her life on a farm.

To Laura and Almanzo, living on the land was the best life they could imagine. They were happy working every day with animals, coaxing the fields and orchards to yield grain and fruit. But Rose called farmwork "slavery to cows and pigs and hens."

Laura was glad for Rose when she began spending time at the railroad station with Ethel Burney. It was good for Rose to have a friend in Mansfield. Ethel's father, Mr. Burney, was the telegraph operator as well as the stationmaster, and he taught the girls Morse code and the operation of the telegraph key.

One fall day Rose came home from town with a determined look on her face. "Mama Bess—I can have a job as a telegraph operator, if I want it."

"Mr. Burney is going to pay you for helping him?" asked Laura. "It's about time."

"I don't mean a job in Mansfield," said Rose in an even more determined voice. "The Western Union main office in Kansas City wants operators. They're paying two dollars and fifty cents a week."

"Kansas City! Rose, you're not eighteen yet. . . . *Two-fifty* a week? My goodness!" Even as Laura was speaking, she remembered something: *She* had not been even sixteen when she had left home for her first teaching job. Rose was just as plucky and adventurous as Laura. It would be cruel to try to keep her in Mansfield, where there were no adventures for bright, ambitious young people. Besides, there was no way for Rose to earn good money in Mansfield.

Not long afterward, Laura helped Rose pack her trunk. Almanzo drove them to the station to take the train for Kansas City, Missouri. In Kansas City, Laura saw Rose settled in a decent boardinghouse, recommended by friends in Mansfield. And then Laura returned home—and Rose was on her own.

Rose was now a "bachelor girl," the new term for young, unmarried working women. She worked as a Western Union telegraph operator at the main office in Kansas City. Before long she also took on the night shift in the Midland Hotel.

In October 1906, Laura visited Rose, now nineteen, in Kansas City. She looked around the Midland Hotel lobby with its white marble, red plush, and glittering chandeliers. This was the kind of luxurious, fast-paced life Rose had read about in books, thought Laura—of course Rose was determined to try it for herself.

Giggling, Rose led her mother up the marble stairs to the women's lounge. "My friend Gladys and I sneak up here and curl our hair. Isn't it like a palace, Mama Bess?" One whole wall was an enormous mirror. There was a row of gleaming white porcelain wash-basins.

"The extravagance!" exclaimed Laura. She turned on the hot water tap at one sink, to make sure the hotel really was wasting all that money heating water just to wash hands. But she couldn't help giggling, too. Alone together with Rose, Laura almost felt as if they were sisters.

When Rose came home to Mansfield for visits, though, Laura couldn't help thinking that her daughter was more out of place there than ever. Mansfield people seemed to think so, too. Laura noticed her neighbors raising their eyebrows at Rose's short (ankle-length) skirts and the independent tilt to her chin.

A few years later, Rose moved out to San Francisco, and then she married a man Laura and Almanzo had never met. Instead of starting a family, Rose made herself a career first in real estate, then in writing for newspapers and magazines. About the same time, Laura

175

found herself launched on a very different kind of writing. It all began with chickens.

"Gingerbread, Laura!" The guests around the dining table at Rocky Ridge took bites of the fragrant cake on their dessert plates. "*I can never make cake this time of year*," said one woman, Emma, "because I never have the eggs. How on earth do you get your hens to lay through the winter?"

Laura exchanged a pleased smile with Almanzo. He knew she was the only chicken farmer in the county who got eggs in the winter, and he was proud of her. "Why, there's nothing to it—I just give them linseed meal before the cold weather sets in, and keep the henhouse extra clean," she told Emma. Modestly she added, "They've asked me to give a little talk on chickens at the farm association meeting next week."

Of course, it wasn't quite true that there was nothing to it. Laura remembered how she'd gotten up before dawn, that frosty morning early in 1911, to carry the buckets of warm mash out to the henhouse. She liked to watch her hens flutter down to the troughs, making little sounds of pleasure even before they began eating.

Laura thought leghorn hens were handsome, with their sleek bodies and their bright red combs. Leghorns might be small, but they were hardy, like Laura herself. And they laid many more eggs than some of the showier breeds of chickens.

When it came time for that particular farm association meeting, Laura decided not to go. There was too much work to do at Rocky Ridge just then. But she had her speech written down, and she asked someone else to read it aloud for her.

One morning a week or so later, Laura kneaded a batch of bread and set the loaves to rise. Then she whistled to the dog to come along and walked down to the road to pick up the mail, as she did every day. In the mailbox, along with the daily newspaper—the *Mansfield Mirror*—there was a letter.

"Why, it's from Mr. Case," she told the dog. "Shall we see what he says?" John Case was the editor of the *Missouri Ruralist,* a twice-a-month farm newspaper. He had heard her speech on raising chickens, the letter said, and he was very impressed. He wanted Laura to contribute to his paper.

Staring at the letter, Laura felt her heart beat faster. She was forty-four. She'd never written anything for publication, except her letter to the De Smet newspaper during the journey from South Dakota to the Ozarks in 1894. But now she hurried back up to the farmhouse, her heart and mind overflowing with what she wanted to write.

While the bread was baking, Laura sat down and wrote her first article for the *Missouri Ruralist.* This piece of writing expressed her joy and pride in the farm she

and Almanzo had built out of almost nothing.

All her life, Laura had loved farm life for the beautiful surroundings—the Wisconsin woods, Plum Creek in Minnesota, and the Dakota prairie. She had planned her farm in the Ozarks, she explained in her article, so that she could enjoy its beauty as she went about her daily life. In the kitchen, she had a window put in over the counter where she kneaded bread. Laura had never liked kneading bread, but she didn't mind it when she could gaze out over the sheep pasture at the same time.

In the living room, four large windows showed off the wooded hills and fields outside. Laura hung curtains at the sides of the windows, but left her "pictures," as she called these outdoor scenes, uncovered. The dining room opened onto a large porch, which was a shady, breezy place to eat on hot summer days.

Laura knew that the readers of the *Missouri Ruralist* were practical, down-to-earth people like her. She pointed out that a small farm, with the right crops and livestock, could provide just as good a living as a large one. Besides, nowadays farming didn't need to be a lonely life like that of a homesteader on the prairies in her childhood. Now, everyone was connected by the telephone. In a community of small farms, farmhouses were closer to one another. People could get together more easily for club meetings and parties.

Also, these days farmwork did not need to be such backbreaking labor. For the first several years at Rocky Ridge, the Wilders had hauled all their water from a spring in the ravine below the house, barns, and henhouse. But then Almanzo built a reservoir at a spring in a pasture above the house and piped the water down to the house. He even ran a pipe through the cookstove in the kitchen so that Laura could have hot and cold running water.

The editor of the *Ruralist,* delighted with

"Favors the Small Farm Home," made it the lead article in the issue of February 18, 1911. Laura was pleased with her success, and she had plenty more to say about Rocky Ridge. Her second article, "The Story of Rocky Ridge Farm," appeared as the lead article in the *Missouri Ruralist* in July 1911.

The next year, Laura wrote another article, "My Apple Orchard," under Almanzo's name. A picture of Almanzo among his apple trees was on the cover of the *Ruralist*. She was proud to see her words in print, to hear praise from her readers, *and* to receive checks for five or ten dollars for each article.

Before long, Laura was the editor of the *Ruralist's* "Home" column. She had an idea, as she mentioned in a letter to her mother, that she might write about her own life. But for the time being, nothing came of that idea.

Out in San Francisco, Rose was doing well, writing for the *San Francisco Bulletin*. But she missed her parents, and she begged Laura to visit. In 1915, the year of the grand Panama-Pacific International Exposition in San Francisco, Rose finally talked Laura into taking the train to California.

During the weeks she stayed in San Francisco, Laura visited the fair several times. The exhibit that impressed her the most was a sculpture, *Pioneer Mother.* Laura and Rose came upon it outside the Palace of the Legion of Honor.

"Oh, Rose," whispered Laura. They gazed up at the bronze life-size group on the pedestal. A woman stood with a sunbonnet hanging down the back of her neck, the way Laura had usually worn her sunbonnet. The sleeves of her dress were rolled up, and her arms curved protectively around her two children. At the same time, she pointed the way forward—westward.

"She might be Grandma Ingalls, mightn't she?" said Rose.

"The details are all so true," said Laura softly. "Look at the shoe. I'd swear it had been half-soled." The shoe sticking out from under the woman's dress was large, heavy, and worn. It was the shoe of a woman who had walked across a continent.

The sight of the sculpture gave Laura a strange, excited feeling. Yes, this "Pioneer Mother" might be Caroline Ingalls, and the girl in the sculpture might be Laura. Now the time of the pioneers—her girlhood—was part of American history, and here was a statue to remind people of it.

"If a sculptor can make a statue of it, you can *write* about it," said Rose. "You should use more experiences from your childhood in your writing."

When Laura returned to Rocky Ridge, she did use some of her girlhood experiences in her columns for the *Missouri Ruralist*. And a few years after World War I ended, she wrote a couple of articles for high-paying national magazines, with Rose's help. But there were always so many other things for Laura to do and think about. She was busy organizing women's study groups, organizing and helping run the Mansfield branch of the National Farm Loan Association, and, of course, doing all the farm chores, including raising her famous chickens. Laura let her writing slide.

While Laura and Almanzo were growing deeper into their farm life in the Ozark Mountains, Rose had gotten divorced and was off having more adventures in the wide world. She traveled in Europe for years at a time. Then, in 1928, Rose came home to Missouri, full of new plans. The stock market was booming, and Rose was flush with money from her investments. "We can't lose!" she told her parents. They had invested with the same stockbroker, on Rose's advice.

Now Rose built a new house at Rocky Ridge, a stone cottage, for Laura and

Almanzo. This way, Rose planned, she could live near her parents, but they would all have their privacy. Rose settled into the old farmhouse, where she rested from her travels and wrote.

Then, in October of 1929, the stock market crashed. Rose lost all her investments. So did Laura and Almanzo. As the Great Depression deepened across the country, Rose fell into a private depression of her own. She could hardly write, and she had a hard time selling what she did write.

Laura had lived through many more bad times than Rose, but this disaster was a blow to her, too. At the same time, the shock jogged something in Laura. She hadn't written any articles, even for the *Missouri Ruralist,* since 1924. But one day early in 1930, she opened her desk and sat down with a pencil and a tablet of cheap lined paper.

Laura's deep blue eyes stared ahead at the cubbyholes in her desk, but her mind's eye saw a horse-drawn covered wagon lumbering across the Kansas prairie. She began to write, in script as neat and even as her sewing stitches: "Once upon a time years and years ago, Pa stopped the horses and the wagon they were hauling away out on the prairie in Indian Territory."

The Little House Books

That spring, as the Great Depression settled like a blight over the country, Laura wrote on about her life as a pioneer girl. She didn't actually remember the Ingallses' year in the log cabin in Indian Territory, but she'd heard the stories so often that she could imagine just the way they'd happened. She wrote about the bright moonlit night Pa had lifted her up to the window, showing her a ring of wolves around the cabin. She wrote about the dangerous river crossing on the way from Kansas back to Wisconsin. She wrote about the time the chimney caught on fire, when she dragged Mary and Baby Carrie away from the flames.

Laura went on with her life at Rocky Ridge as usual, planting the vegetable garden and meeting with her friends and mixing up her special feed for the chickens. But in spare moments, while soup simmered on the stove or between hanging out the wash and starting dinner, she would pick up her pencil and step back into the world of her childhood. Laura wrote about the first home she did remember, the little house in the Big Woods of Wisconsin. She wrote about quarrels with her sister Mary, and about making maple syrup. She wrote about all the close calls they'd had with bears, prairie fires, blizzards, stampeding cattle, the flooding creek.

As Laura's pencil scurried over the lined paper, the music of Pa's fiddle filled her head. She wrote about cozy winter evenings and hopeful spring sunrises. She wrote about the good taste of rabbit stew cooked over a campfire on the prairie, and ripe wild plums picked from the creek bottom.

At the beginning of May, when Rocky Ridge was lovely with ferns and wildflowers, Laura finished the story of her childhood. She walked over the hill from the stone cottage to the farmhouse and handed the stack of school tablets to Rose.

"'Pioneer Girl'!" exclaimed Rose as she ran her eyes over the first lined page. "Good! It's about time you wrote down your pioneer experiences." Rose typed Laura's manuscript to send around to magazines. She also copied some of Charles Ingalls's stories from the manuscript and put them together as a picture book, to offer to children's book publishers.

Months went by, and no one seemed interested in publishing the story of Laura's childhood. Then, one morning in February 1931, when Rose was away on a trip to New York, Laura walked down to the road with Nero, the dog, to get the mail. There in the mailbox was a letter from a children's book publisher. Laura's breath caught in her throat as she ripped open the envelope.

It seemed that they liked Laura's stories about the Big Woods very much. "It covers a period in American history about which very little has been written, and almost nothing for boys and girls," wrote the children's book editor. But they wanted Laura to completely rewrite the story.

The editor thought Laura's story should be not a picture book but a full-length novel for eight-to-twelve-year-olds. It should include a lot of details and descriptions about pioneer life: exactly what the people wore, how they made butter, how Pa molded his own bullets, what kinds of games the children played. Oh, and the book needed a better title.

Laura felt thrilled and overwhelmed at the same time. The editor liked her story very much! But—*rewrite the whole thing?*

A few days later, another letter arrived from Rose in New York. She had gone to talk to the editor herself. The editor was "crazy" about Laura's writing, Rose said. "Everyone is who has seen it. She says you make such perfect pictures of everything, and that the characters are all absolutely *real.*"

In her enthusiastic way, Rose told Laura just what to do. She should buy some more lined tablets and sit down and write another fifteen thousand words about the Ingalls family's life in the Big Woods. The story should cover one year, all four seasons. When Rose came home from New York, she would edit and type the new story.

Once again, Laura spent the spring writing. To her surprise, her memories seemed even deeper and richer the second time around. She realized why she needed to describe all the details of her early life: because life was so different for children now. Her book would show them how closely young Laura and her family had lived with the rhythm of the seasons.

In the fall, the Ingalls family smoked venison and stored the harvest. In the winter, the girls made thimble pictures in the frost on the window, and the family drove the sleigh to visit relatives. In the spring, Pa plowed and they planted a garden. Summer, when the cow gave the most milk, was the time to make cheese.

Writing about her childhood made Laura homesick for De Smet and her family—what was left of it. Ma had died in 1924, and Mary in 1928. Laura and Almanzo had wanted to travel to South Dakota in the summer of 1930, to celebrate their forty-fifth wedding anniversary, but they couldn't afford it. In 1931, they were finally able to take the trip to De Smet. Instead of going for their wedding anniversary, on August 25, they went for Old Settlers Day, June 10.

The Wilders retraced the route they had

followed from South Dakota to Missouri so many years ago. Once again the prairies were suffering heat and drought, and the farmers were in the grip of the depression. But at least this time, the trip took only several days instead of six weeks. Instead of a horse-drawn wagon, they drove a blue Buick, with their dog Nero perched on the running board.

In De Smet, Laura was struck with how long ago her childhood now seemed. She had seen times change in Missouri—for instance, the hitching-posts in town where farmers used to tie their horses had been taken down in the 1920s. But somehow she had still been thinking of De Smet as a town where everyone drove wagons or buggies.

Before they returned to Missouri, Laura and Almanzo drove west to the Black Hills of Dakota, where they visited Carrie. Laura told Carrie how she felt about seeing De Smet again. "Our childhood is slipping away. I feel that I must remember exactly how it used to be.

I must write it *all* down, before it's lost forever."

At the end of March 1932, Laura's first copies of *Little House in the Big Woods* arrived at Rocky Ridge. Almost running, Laura hurried over the hill to the farmhouse to show the newborn book to Rose. Together they marveled at the pen-and-ink drawings, like illustrations for a folktale. They gloried in the way the stories read on the page, so smooth and book-like. "Very well done," said Rose. "You're an author, Mama Bess!"

Laura smiled. "I know," she said. She was already launched on a second book.

Everyone loved *Little House in the Big Woods,* it seemed. The Junior Literary Guild chose Laura's book for its April 1932 selection. Reviewers couldn't say enough good things about it: "Refreshingly genuine and lifelike"; "delightful and absorbing"; "treasurable." On top of that, Laura's first royalty check was five hundred dollars.

Laura was especially glad that she had enough money so she could send some to her sister Grace. Grace and her husband were desperately poor, and Grace's health was bad. Carrie wrote Laura that Grace was in the hospital with severe diabetes. Visiting Grace, Carrie had read *Little House in the Big Woods* aloud, and they had enjoyed it together.

Now that Laura had discovered how satisfying it was to write a book, she wasn't about to stop. Even before *Little House in the Big Woods* was published, she had started working on a second book. This one was about Almanzo's childhood in upstate New York. As she wrote, she checked facts with Almanzo, and she drew diagrams of the Wilder farmhouse and barns and fields. She tried to get her husband to talk about things that had happened to him as a boy.

Almanzo was good with facts, but almost no help with the stories. "I'm not much of a hand to tell a story," he protested.

"A hand!" retorted Laura. "No, you're certainly not a hand—you're more like an *oyster,* the way I have to pry every little thing out of you. Thank goodness that Royal told me about the time you fed taffy to your little pig, and she ran all over the farm with you chasing her. And that Alice told me about the time you threw the stove polish brush at her and made a big splotch on the parlor wallpaper, and you thought you'd get a whipping but Alice mended the wallpaper so your folks never knew."

Almanzo chuckled at the memories, but he still didn't say much.

Alice had also told Laura about the time the big rough boys tried to beat up the nice young schoolteacher in Malone. Laura hoped to get more details from Almanzo, but he only answered "yes" or "no" in his maddening way. So she filled in the descriptions from her memory of the school in Burr Oak.

Laura remembered so clearly how that

huge, loutish boy had swaggered down the aisle toward her beloved teacher, Mr. Reed. She remembered the sick feeling in her stomach. It must have been like that for Almanzo, although he didn't say so.

Laura knew now that readers were eagerly waiting for as many books as she could turn out. Many children wrote letters to tell her so. In April 1933, a boy in Iowa wrote: "I wish this year would hurry so I could read your new book, *Farmer Boy*. I read *Little House in the Big Woods* twice. It helped us in our pioneer study a lot. We made butter like you did when you were a little girl."

Before *Farmer Boy* was published later in 1933, Laura had decided what her third book would be. She wanted to tell the story of the year the Ingalls family spent on the Kansas prairie, in Indian Territory. Because she'd been too young to remember that year, she made a special effort to research the facts for this book. She and Rose even drove to Kansas to see if they could find the site of the log cabin Pa had built.

Laura wasn't able to find the exact place where the Ingalls house had stood on the Kansas prairie. But she learned a great deal about how much Kansas had changed. As Laura and Rose neared Independence, they were amazed to see oil wells on the horizon.

Oil wells, where once pioneers had homesteaded! This was another sign that Laura had better write down, as soon as she could, what life had been like for a pioneer girl. She needed to capture the scent of wild roses on the prairie, the taste of corn bread baked over a campfire, the thrill of meeting a wolf under the stars on a frozen lake.

Now working on *High Prairie*, as Laura and Rose called the new book, Laura was learning more and more about the craft of writing. It was not enough for Laura to say, "This is exactly what happened," and write it down. The real incidents of her life needed to be shaped into stories that fit together in a satisfying way.

Laura had already partly realized that, while working on *Little House in the Big Woods*. It made a better story if the Ingallses had lived in Wisconsin from the time Mary was born until the time Laura was five or six. But then she had to make other changes—for instance, Carrie would have to be born in Wisconsin, instead of Kansas.

Planning the books to come, Laura and Rose wanted the series to fit together as one long story. In real life, the Ingallses had moved from Wisconsin to Kansas, back to Wisconsin, on to Minnesota, then back east to Burr Oak, and then back west to the same town in Minnesota. But it made a more powerful—and less confusing—story for the family to move steadily from east to west.

There were so many things that would have to be left out because they didn't fit in. It worked better if the Ingallses in the stories had only one dog, the faithful Jack, through several books. Of course in real life, Pa had given Jack to the man who bought his horses, Pet and Patty, on the journey from Kansas. And after the family was settled in the Big Woods again, they'd gotten a new puppy, Wolf.

So Wolf, the frisky young dog who'd chewed the mitten Laura had knit for Baby Carrie, had to be left out of Laura's books entirely. In fact, the incident itself had to be left out. Jack, a dignified, older dog, never would have stolen and chewed the mitten.

By early 1934, Laura had finished writing *High Prairie*. That September, *Little House on the Prairie* (the final name for *High Prairie*) was published. Everyone liked it just as much as they had the first two books. "Mrs. Wilder has caught the very essence of pioneer life," said one reviewer.

Laura went on to write about the years in

Walnut Grove, Minnesota, on the banks of Plum Creek. Again, she made some changes to turn what had really happened into a better story. She combined the two hateful girls of her childhood, Nellie Owens and Genevieve Masters, into one unpleasant character, "Nellie Oleson."

Making an even bigger change, Laura decided to leave out the entire year in Burr Oak. She didn't want to tell about her brother Freddie's death and of the sad journey to Iowa. She didn't want to explain that the Ingallses had been so poor at the end of that year, they'd had to sneak out of town without paying the rent.

No, thought Laura, it was too harsh a story for children. So in *On the Banks of Plum Creek*, the Ingalls family stayed in Minnesota, instead of moving to Iowa and back again. Grace was born in Minnesota, not Iowa.

In March 1936, Laura wrote the last page of *On the Banks of Plum Creek*. She wrapped up the lined tablets of her manuscript in brown paper, tied the package with string, and sent it to Rose. Rose was now living in Columbia, the capital of Missouri, doing research for a book about the state. So instead of walking over the hill from the rock house to the farmhouse to consult with each other, Laura and Rose wrote letters back and forth.

To help Rose work on the book, Laura drew a map of Plum Creek. She showed the dugout where the Ingallses had lived at first, the sod barn, and the huge gray rock where she and Mary had played. She put in the new house Pa had built on the other side of the creek, the new barn, and the vegetable garden. She noted the directions to the Nelsons' farm and to the town of Walnut Grove.

It amazed Laura that the more she thought about her girlhood, the more she remembered. Those times became so vivid in her mind that it was almost like living them over again. Sometimes Rose had to remind her that her readers needed her to write down all the details that were so clear to her. "I see the pictures so plainly that I guess I failed to paint them as I should," she wrote Rose. Laura needed to describe life on the prairie for readers who couldn't see the scenes for themselves. She had to be their eyes, the way she'd been Mary's eyes after she became blind.

Laura was grateful for Rose's help. And she had great faith in Rose, a professional writer, to decide what would make the best story. "You know your judgment is better than mine," she wrote, "so what you decide is the one that stands."

But sometimes Laura had to correct Rose's revisions, because she knew her characters so well. Once Rose had Ma say "she vowed she didn't believe those young ones were *ever* going to sleep." Laura knew Ma was so ladylike that she would never even "vow" anything. She wouldn't call children "young ones," either— that would have sounded uneducated.

＊ ＊ ＊ ＊

After her work in Columbia was done, Rose decided not to move back to Rocky Ridge. So in the fall of 1936, after several years in the stone cottage, Laura and Almanzo moved back into their beloved farmhouse.

The next year, *On the Banks of Plum Creek* was published. Again, the reviews were enthusiastic. "A warm, glowing picture of steadfast family love and devotion," said *The Horn Book,* a journal of children's literature. The best reviews, though, were letters to Laura from children, asking when the next book was coming out.

Rose was working on a new book of her own, for adults, about pioneer life. This novel was based on Laura and Almanzo's first four years of homesteading in South Dakota. Rose had many questions for her parents, more than they could answer. To get Rose more information, Laura wrote to Grace, hoping her memory would fill in some blanks.

Grace wrote back with the names of prairie wildflowers: crocuses, wild peas, tiger lilies, wild geraniums. "To think that I could have forgotten all this which comes back to me now," Laura wrote Rose. "That's why the sooner I write my stuff the better."

Laura hadn't intended to write about the early years of her marriage, when she and Almanzo had survived one disaster after another. But now that Rose was writing a novel about these events, Laura felt an urge to put down her own version. She wrote a complete manuscript about those first four years. But she had doubts about whether it would sell, and whether it was a good idea to publish this story, after all. In the end, it stayed in the bottom of a drawer.

"I Love You, Laura"

By 1937, Laura had written her fifth children's book, *By the Shores of Silver Lake*. It was about the Ingallses' move from Walnut Grove, Minnesota, to the Dakota Territory. While Rose edited *By the Shores of Silver Lake,* Laura began the book she called *The Hard Winter.* They wrote back and forth to get the details right and to decide how to shape the books.

Now that Laura was writing about her life in De Smet, she wanted to refresh her memory of the place. She and Almanzo planned to drive there again in the spring of 1938. But this time they would first travel across the country, all the way to California. On the way back, they would visit Laura's sisters.

In South Dakota, Laura and Almanzo stopped first at Keystone, in the Black Hills, to visit Carrie. Driving east to Manchester, the Wilders visited Grace and her husband. In nearby De Smet, they enjoyed seeing old friends. Laura took note of what her "Little Town on the Prairie" was like, and she thought about how it used to be.

After returning to Rocky Ridge, Laura got back to work on the book she was calling *The Hard Winter.* (The title was later changed to *The Long Winter,* because the editor thought the story was already grim enough.) Laura and Rose had discussed a plan for the story.

But Laura didn't agree with Rose that George Masters and his wife should be left in the story. Rose's idea was that a baby being born in the midst of the settlers' struggle to survive would be a hopeful touch. In Laura's opinion, however, the Masters family had taken up much too much room in the Ingallses' home during the legendary winter of 1880 to 1881. Laura didn't intend to give them any room in her story. What she wanted to emphasize was Cap Garland's and Almanzo's courage in hauling the wheat that saved the town from starving.

By May 1939, Laura had finished *The Long Winter.* She sent it to Rose, who was now living in Danbury, Connecticut.

At first, Laura had planned to write only two more books in the Little House series after *By the Shores of Silver Lake.* But now she realized that she needed two more books after *The Long Winter.* She wanted to get in all her stories about going to school and teaching school herself, and about her courtship with Almanzo.

Little Town on the Prairie was published toward the end of 1941. Grace died about the same time, and Laura was so glad that she had visited her sister one more time in 1939.

In the spring of 1943, *Those Happy Golden Years* was published. When Laura received her copies of this last book in the series, she inscribed one book with a verse especially for Rose:

> *And so farewell to childhood days*
> *Their joys, and hopes, and fears.*
> *But Father's voice and his fiddle's*
> > *song*
> *Go echoing down the years.*

Laura's saga of her pioneer girlhood was complete.

As usual, reviewers showered praise on Laura's books. "A moving and authentic re-creation of American frontier life," said *The New Yorker* magazine of *Little Town on the Prairie*. "There is in these books about Laura and her people the freshness and vigor of pioneer America, of the days where there was land to claim beyond the Mississippi," *The Saturday Review* said of *Those Happy Golden Years.*

Around the same time that *Little Town on the Prairie* came out, Japan bombed Pearl Harbor. The United States plunged into World War II. Laura had been born two years after the end of the *Civil War*! Her childhood was indeed far back in American history.

In the summer of 1947, the illustrator Garth Williams came to Rocky Ridge to visit Laura. Almanzo picked him up at the train station in his Chrysler, and Laura greeted him at the door of the farmhouse. "Mr. Williams! I'm so honored that you're doing the new illustrations for my books. I love your drawings for Mr. White's *Charlotte's Web* and *Stuart Little.*"

Taking off his hat, Garth Williams shook Laura's hand. "Mrs. Wilder, *I'm* greatly honored to illustrate the Little House books. I want to get everything just right. I've visited the Big Woods and the Kansas prairie and Plum Creek and De Smet, and now I need to check some points with you."

They sat on the porch with glasses of lemonade. The illustrator took drawings from his portfolio, asking Laura question after question. As they talked, the bulldog, Ben, came to Laura and put his head in her lap.

Glancing up, Garth Williams noticed Almanzo walking toward the barn. The old farmer walked with a cane, but he carried a pitchfork over his shoulder. "Does Mr. Wilder still do farm chores?"

"Yes, he has a little herd of goats." Laura rubbed Ben behind the ears. "Manly's doing fairly well for a man who turned ninety this year, don't you think?" Her voice was warm with pride. "He milks the goats by hand, and I churn all our own butter from the goat milk."

But two years later, in July 1949, Almanzo suffered a heart attack. Laura nursed him for several weeks, and gradually he got better. Then early one Sunday morning in October, he had a second heart attack. Laura saw him slump into an armchair. She grabbed the phone and called for help.

The neighbors arrived soon afterward, but Almanzo had died. Laura sat in the armchair with her arms around her husband of sixty-four years.

Tomorrow morning, thought Laura, when she brought up the mail from the mailbox at the road, she would have to read it by herself. She could no longer go out to Almanzo's workshop and read him letters from Rose or friends in De Smet. There would be no more evenings of cribbage games or companionable reading. Next spring, Almanzo would not appear at the kitchen door with a bouquet of the wildflowers she loved.

Rose came from Connecticut for Almanzo's funeral and stayed with her mother for a few weeks afterward. Laura was glad to have Rose with her, but she missed Almanzo terribly. Nothing could change that.

"Do you think you might sell the farm and move into town now?" asked Rose one morning over breakfast. "You'd be near friends, and near shopping."

Laura knew that Rose was concerned about her. "You think I'd be less lonely in town. But I'm lonely because I miss Manly." She had to pause for a moment, because the loneliness hurt as if her chest were bruised inside. "If I left Rocky Ridge, I'd miss him just as much— and besides that, I'd miss Rocky Ridge."

As the years went on, Rose came to Missouri for long visits, often around Thanksgiving or Christmas. Rose was the only family Laura had left now, and she was always delighted to have her company. But all her life Laura had enjoyed her own company, and she was content to spend most of her time by herself, reading, sewing, and listening to the radio, or playing solitaire.

Laura was still lively and cheerful, glad to see friends when they stopped by. She could quote poetry from her wide reading over the years, and she kept up with world affairs through reading the newspapers. On Sunday afternoons, friends would take Laura for a drive. Every day the neighbor boys brought Laura's mail—including fan letters and royalty checks—up from the road.

On Wednesdays, a hired driver picked Laura up and took her into town to shop and go to the bank and the library. She was always nicely dressed in her old-fashioned style, wearing high-button black shoes and a hat. Blue was her favorite color, and she often wore handmade lace around her neck.

Laura's friends on the library staff saved new books for her—she especially enjoyed Western novels. She would stop in at the *Mansfield Mirror* and chat with the editor about goings-on around town. Then she'd have lunch at a café.

Besides writing Laura letters, many of her fans actually came to see her. They came from all over the country—one day, she had visitors from New York, Pennsylvania, and California. Another day, she was startled to find fans at her door at seven o'clock in the morning.

Even though she was in her eighties now, Laura was still ready for new adventures. One year, Rose persuaded Laura to come back east with her, since Laura had never visited Rose's Connecticut house. She and Laura flew—Laura's first airplane ride.

Honors kept on coming to Laura. In Detroit, a new library was named after her. In 1950, a children's reading room was dedicated to her in far-off Pomona, California. In 1951, her own town of Mansfield decided to name their library after her. Laura attended the dedication ceremony in her best dress, a dark red velvet. She also wore this dress next year to a bookstore in Springfield during Children's Book Week.

This autograph party was her last public appearance.

In 1953, the new edition of the Little House books with Garth Williams's illustrations was finally published. Laura had liked the original illustrations, but these realistic drawings touched her deeply. She sent her publisher a telegram: "Laura and Mary and their folks live again in these illustrations."

The next year, the Children's Library Association established the Laura Ingalls Wilder Award. Laura was the first to receive this medal, given every five years to an author who "has made a substantial and lasting contribution to literature for children." Of course this described the Little House books exactly.

Laura's good health continued until the last two years of her life. She was determined that she would live to be ninety, at least, since Almanzo had. But when Rose came to Rocky Ridge for Thanksgiving in 1957, she found Laura very ill. At the Springfield hospital, they discovered she had diabetes. Rose stayed with her mother through the next two months.

Laura got her wish about turning ninety. On February 10, 1957, just a few days after her ninetieth birthday, she died at home. She left a note for Rose, to whom she had willed everything. The note ended, "My love will be with you always."

Over the years, the Little House books have become beloved by one generation of children after another. Fans couldn't get enough of Laura and her family. After her mother's death, Rose discovered Laura's diary of the Wilders' journey from South Dakota to Missouri in 1894. She wrote an Introduction and a Conclusion for it, and this book was published in 1962 as *On the Way Home*.

After Rose died in 1968, Laura's manuscript about her early married life was found in a box of old papers. It was published under the title of *The First Four Years* in 1971. In

1974, the letters Laura wrote Almanzo during her trip to San Francisco in 1915 were published as *West from Home: Letters of Laura Ingalls Wilder to Almanzo Wilder, San Francisco 1915.*

Meanwhile, in 1974, the TV series *Little House on the Prairie* was launched. The series didn't have much connection with Laura's books or her actual life, but it was very popular and ran for several years.

All kinds of spin-offs, including Little House songbooks, cookbooks, and dolls, continue to appear. Laura's original stories have been adapted as picture books or first chapter books. Several different writers have written new books about Ma's childhood, and Grandma's childhood, and Rose's childhood, in the style of the Little House books. As for the Little House books themselves, over sixty million copies have been sold.

The story Laura told in her books was the story of her own family. But even more, it was the story of America. "Running through all the stories, like a golden thread, is the same thought of the values of life," Laura once described her books. These values were "courage, self-reliance, independence, integrity and helpfulness. Cheerfulness and humor were handmaids to courage."

This is the way Americans are proud to think of themselves—this is the pioneer spirit at its best. Laura's vision of the American pioneer adventure continues to inspire readers, and they treasure her for it. At the autograph party in Springfield in 1952, the Springfield children's librarian had showed Laura the library's copy of one of the Little House books. It had been read almost to pieces. On the last page a message was scrawled, in a child's handwriting, "I love you, Laura."

Books by Laura Ingalls Wilder

Little House in the Big Woods, 1932
Farmer Boy, 1933
Little House on the Prairie, 1935
On the Banks of Plum Creek, 1937
By the Shores of Silver Lake, 1939
The Long Winter, 1940
Little Town on the Prairie, 1941
Those Happy Golden Years, 1943
On the Way Home, 1962
The First Four Years, 1971
West from Home, 1974